MERLIN'S HARP

MERLIN'S HARP

Anne Eliot Crompton

DONALD I. FINE, INC.

New York

Library of Congress Catalogue Card Number: 95-060938

ISBN: 1-55611-463-X

Manufactured in the United States of America

10   9   8   7   6   5   4   3   2   1

Designed by Irving Perkins Associates

This novel is a work of fiction. Names, characters, places and incidents are
either the product of the author's imagination or are used fictiously. Any
resemblance to actual events, locales, organizations or persons, living or
dead, is entirely coincidental and beyond the intent of either the
author or publisher.

Acknowledgment

Geoffrey Ashe, in his book *The Discovery of King Arthur,* suggests that the reason the historian Gildas never mentioned King Arthur by name was, that Arthur had robbed Christian monastaries for his war chests. (Gildas wrote judgmental history.) This exciting theory became a pillar of *Merlin's Harp*.

—ANNE ELIOT COMPTON

A Counsel Oak Leaf Song

Water rising under rock
Breaks earth's lock,
Floods thirsty roots,
Nurtures sap and trunk and shoots,
Greens and plumps each greedy leaf
Till dappled sunlight like a thief
Sucks leaf-water as I breathe,
Makes of mist an airy wreath
To drift and float and wander high
To the sky,
And fall again,
Sweet, rich rain,
Run under rock and
Rise again.

1

MERLIN'S HARP

When I was yet a very young woman I threw my heart away.

I fashioned a wee coracle of leaf and willow twig and reed, a coracle that sat in the hollow of my two palms. In this I placed my wounded, wretched heart, and I set it adrift on the rain-misted wavelets of the Fey river, and I watched it bob and whirl, sail and sink. Ever since then I have lived heartless, or almost heartless, cold as spring rain, the way Humans think all Fey live. Humans I have known would be astounded to learn that I ever had a heart that leapt, brightened, fainted, quickened, warmed, embraced, froze or rejected, like their own.

I grew up in a strangely Human way in a home, with a sort of family. My mother Nimway, my brother Lugh and I lived in Lady Villa on Apple Island, which Human bards have named Avalon. I say we "lived" there. Most nights we slept within the villa walls. We cooked many a meal over the stone circle fireplace in the villa courtyard. When we sought each others' company we looked in the villa, in certain of the old rooms, a special room for each of us. My mother's room had faded waves painted on its walls, and strange, leaping fish, such as we never caught in the Fey lake. My small room was painted about with vines—unlike those that clung to and camouflaged the villa walls—and clusters of purple fruits. Because of these pictures, Lugh and I always believed that there were worlds beyond the Fey forest, where mysterious creatures lived. Few Fey children grow up knowing that.

Like other children, I went away to join the Children's Guard as soon as I could care for myself. But unlike other children, I remembered the villa as my home, I remembered the Lady, my mother, and I always knew that Lugh, the big, pale boy who often stood guard with me, was my born brother. We had sucked the same breasts and learned to walk on the same cool, tiled floor. We were special to each other, as no other two children were.

And though I never said so till our Guard time ended, and then only to my best friend, Elana, I always knew that when I grew up and left the Guard I would go home.

The villa grew about us and entwined our lives as vines entwined the villa. Apple Island held us apart from mainland Fey forest and our silent, Fey neighbors. Living on the mainland we would have glimpsed neighbors from afar, as we glimpse other wild creatures; by slow, easy approaches we would have come to know many of them by name, and some as friends. But the lake trapped us, for the most part, with each other.

Living like this, as in a Human family, I grew an almost Human-like heart. This was a deformity. Even on the bright spring morning when I climbed Counsel Oak with my best friend Elana, I knew I could not live much longer with this heart.

The Lady, who knew so much, must have known I had it.

Elana knew. She did not mind because she had a heart too. In truth, hers was bigger and warmer than mine, and fast growing desperate. I could have had no notion how desperate, for such intensity had no precursor in our Fey world.

Counsel Oak towers over all the apple trees of Avalon. At that time his massive trunk yawned half open where it had been split by a bolt from heaven, long ago. A lesser tree would have drooped and dropped and given back its life to the Goddess. But the young oak that we would call Counsel reared on up, seeking the sun.

Up we climbed, Elana and I, from huge branch to smaller branch, past new leaf and mistletoe, through thrush song and warbler flight. A few days before we had left the Children's Guard at last, still wrapped in the "invisible" cloaks in which Guards spy from treetop and thicket on the Human kingdom beyond our forest. We had lingered a bit, building shelters and scavenging. Then I had said to Elana, "Come home with me." And Elana had come.

I perched now in the highest crotch that would bear my very slight weight. Elana settled lower, for she was a big girl; she carried real weight. Together we looked out over all of Apple Island, and the Fey lake with its dark, encircling forest, and the small, shimmering streams that fed the lake, and the wide river that flowed away east to the kingdom.

Uncounted white-blooming apple trees crowded the island below us. The trees hid Avalon's two dwelling dens, but I knew where they were. Otter Mellias' newly built cabin stood on stilts over the water on the east shore. Lady Villa crouched among willows on the west shore. Had we climbed Counsel Oak in times long past we could have seen the villa from here. It would have shone out at us, dazzled us, white stone among bright gardens. We might have seen giant, Human figures like those painted on the villa walls stride across the courtyard, or talk beside the fountain. The fountain spat water back then, so the Lady said.

Elana whistled like a blackbird. I looked down and saw her raise plump hands in silent sign-talk. She signed, *Listen to the leaves.*

I had told her that Counsel's rustling leaves gave advice. So the Lady said. Now I listened to the leaves, but heard no words. I shrugged.

Elana looked sadly up at me, her round face white as the apple blossoms below. Her red-brown braid lay against a bough like sun-spattered bark. She signed, *Ask! Ask the Oak: will he notice me now?*

I signed down, *Who? Will who notice you?*

Almost frantically, *He! The one I long for!*

I sighed. We had discussed this "one" before now. I believed my friend must be bewitched, like a Human heroine in some bardic song. In all the forest there was only one for her. If he lay with her, then she would bloom like spring. If he scorned her she feared to wilt clean away. Meantime, she had lain with no one, not ever, not even at the Flowering Moon dances, though we were both now blood-blessed by the Goddess. The same was true of me, but for no such weird reason.

Again I listened to the wind in Counsel's leaves; and this time I thought I heard a distant whisper. *Down.*

I signed to Elana, *Down. That's all the leaves say. Down.*

Listen again, Niviene!

Listening once more, I thought I heard, *Maiden. Down.*

And then soft, far voices sang together,

Maiden, look down.
Look down, Maiden.
Down, down,
Adownderry, look down.

So it was true, what the Lady said! Counsel Oak's leaves gave counsel. But he told us what he wished us to know, not what we asked. I leaned over and around and looked down through leaves and mistletoe. And down there among the ancient apple trees, I saw a shining mystery.

It stood tall alone by itself, as no Fey would ever stand. Disdaining shielding shadow, it gleamed in full sunshine, obvious as a tree—or as a Human, who thinks his own kind kings of the world.

Once I had seen a red stag stand like that, careless and proud; and his summer coat had shone with that same bronze tint. The East Edge Children's Guard had feasted on him for days and days.

I twirled my "invisible" cloak around me and started down the oak, hand under hand. I passed Elana lifting her fingers to ask, *What? Where?* and slipped down the trunk like a shadow. Above me I heard the soft shiftings of Elana's weight as she followed. Dropping to earth I slunk, crouching, from one gray-green trunk to the next, snuffling up hints like a vixen. My nose soon told me that was no stag ahead. I smelled smoke, dust, a body washed seldom, and certainly not recently. A body fed on meat. I paused behind an alder thicket and peered through.

Against an apple trunk leaned a very tall, very pale maiden. Her height was surprising, and so was her skin: milk-white, like Elana's, and gold-freckled. She raised a thin, empty face to the sky. One of her hip-length bronze braids had fallen loose. The other was still held by a shiny red ribbon, which wound around and down its length.

I saw only her radiance. Forgetting all sense and the strong testimony of my nose, I thought, Here is the Goddess herself! In that unforgettable moment I felt what Humans feel when they glimpse one of us. I shrank together. Mouth dry, hair stiff, I crouched beneath her pale gaze, still as hare beneath circling hawk. Since then, because of that unforgotten moment, I have dealt gently with many an innocent Human.

Elana's breath blew hot on my neck. At least I did not face the Goddess alone! One of my kind breathed on me and gripped my shoulder with a slightly shaking, heavy hand.

My friend Elana was bigger, heavier, than I was, but not stronger. Elana had no sliver, no crumb or morsel of magic in all her awkward body or childish mind. I crouched between her and the Goddess. I felt I must protect her from the Goddess. She was my friend. I had to face the Goddess for both of us.

I collected my mind, snatched back some sense, paid heed to my nose. I noticed that the Goddess' white tunic, which should shine like the sun, was deeply soil-grimed. Her overgown, wondrously blue and richly embroidered, was bramble-shredded, her slender white wrists bramble-blooded. I saw by her wide, vague eyes that

7

she was heavily drugged. Dirt! said my nose, Meat! Mead! Grand Mushroom! A great breath of relief filled my lungs. This was no Goddess.

Then, what was it?

A female Human, that's what it was. A Human, naturally taller than myself, but not much older; thin, drugged, unarmed. Not so much as a knife poked out of her brightly embroidered girdle. Her freckled hands hung, helpless.

A female Human stood under the blooming trees of Apple Island, where no Human foot had trod since the Romans went away (so said the Lady). And I, young Niviene, recently a Child Guard, had found her! What would the Lady do if she crouched in my place?

I rose up and walked around the alders. Behind me, Elana gasped. Calmly I approached the prey till my nose nearly touched her breast. Calmly I looked up into her rain-grey eyes. I said, "Woman, what are you doing here?"

Her eyes widened. The pupils nearly covered the iris. She had feasted richly on Grand Mushroom—or, more likely, someone had feasted her. Slowly she drew herself up to her full, impressive height and spoke strange words. They rustled past me like the wind in Counsel's leaves. I said, "What?" And then my ears repeated the words, and I knew they were Latin. Because of the Lady's friend Merlin, his harp and his songs, I knew a little Latin.

She said again in Latin, "Rude boy! Tell me where I am."

She did not know! It was not her doing that she stood on Apple Island, magic-guarded home of the Lady, home of me, Niviene.

I flashed a grin up at her, open-mouthed. This gesture displayed my sharp-filed canine teeth to full advantage. This gesture should show her beyond all doubt where she stood, and in what danger.

With sudden, sure knowledge I said, "Otter Mellias brought you here!"

At my shoulder, Elana murmured, "The Otter! Of course! Who else?"

Only he could have done this. Only Mellias, who dared live on Apple Island near the dangerous Lady, would have dared seize and drug this Human, roll her into a coracle (with the help of merry friends, no doubt) and pole her over here where no Human had set foot since the Romans. He would have done it for spiteful fun— more fun than spite. Anyone else who snatched a Human girl at dusk from a Fey forest edge would have played with her, then left her body in a thicket. Only the Otter would imagine this escapade.

Mellias was young, like my brother; not long out of the Guard; brown and cheerful as an otter. Over on the mainland I used to spy on him as he entertained his many friends with song and story, or invented new steps for the Flowering Moon dance, or worked up new tunes on his pipe.

When Mellias came over to the island and built his heron-nest cabin, I swam over one evening from the Guard and sneaked in. Mellias was fishing off his deck, back turned to the inner cabin. I fluttered like a moth from neat bedroll to neatly hung bow, sling, javelin, ax, to neatly folded shirts, trousers, cloak. I marveled at the ordered space in that cabin, the respectful care of things. Under the folded trousers I found a small crystal. Most Fey keep some such protective device, even if they know no magic. My hand closed on this and lifted it away, even as I drifted like a breeze out the curtained door. Even now, Mellias' crystal swung on a thong from my neck.

I grinned up at my Human. Her head lolled back against the apple trunk. She murmured, "Arthur will come."

I shook my head till my black braid swung. No one would come.

"Mark me. Arthur will come."

Her knees gave way. She sank down the trunk with a slow ripping sound as the blue overgown tore on the bark, and she landed in a half-conscious heap. Down there on the cool earth in the shade her aura showed up: a narrow, pale green flicker, strongest in the areas of the heart and genitals. Grand Mushroom had dimmed and dulled it, but I suspected it had never been strong or bright.

I knelt down and took the large, pale Human hand in my small, dark one. I had touched Human hands before, and was not surprised to find it warmly alive like my own.

Elana squatted and touched the loose ribbon-bound braid. She touched lightly at first, then her fist closed on the braid as she worked to bring the red ribbon free. It came hard, and the woman whimpered, "What are you doing?"

Elana bit her plump lip and pulled. Out came the knife from her belt and sliced the ribbon in three places. It slid off the braid.

The helpless woman muttered, "Arthur will drown you."

I said, "The blue gown is nice. Enough for two shirts."

"Torn," Elana remarked. "Dirty."

"The girdle."

"Aha!" Elana sliced the girdle in half without harming the white body—or even the tunic—under it, and we pulled it from under the woman's weight.

"Enough," said Elana. I looked at the stained white tunic. "No," said Elana, "it's filthy." She was right. Also, there were little rips running through it. It had not been woven or sewn for forest wear.

The woman said in clear Latin, "Arthur will drown both you witches."

"What are those words she says?" Elana asked me.

"Latin. She talks Latin." Elana had never heard Merlin's Human songs or ancient stories.

"Does she understand what we say?"

"I doubt it."

"Ah." Elana looked down at the now unconscious form with a new sort of interest. If the woman could not talk to us or understand us, she was not even of Human value; she was a wounded wild creature we had found. Elana suggested, "We could eat her."

I said, "Leave her to Mellias." He was the hunter.

But I laid hold of her loose braid and pulled from it three bronze strands, each finer than the finest wool thread ever seen. These I braided together and thrust into my pouch. Elana asked me why I did this. I could only shrug. Sometimes my spirit told me to do things, and I did them, not knowing why.

I rose. Elana crouched a moment more, looking up at me, and I noticed how like she looked to our victim: the same pale skin (though not as pale), light hair, tall build. It was not the first time I had thought Elana might have Human blood.

She stood up, holding the cut pieces of ribbon and girdle. We wrapped our invisible cloaks carefully about us and stepped away, moving from shadow to shadow, breaking no twig.

Behind us, the tall white woman in the white tunic lay heaped under the apple tree, breathing as though asleep. She was no threat to us or Apple Island, or the Fey forest. When Mellias finished with her he would make sure of that.

Flitting past Counsel Oak I heard his leaves murmur a name: *Arthur.*

I had heard that name before, long ago. I had heard it whispered in the night when Merlin and the Lady thought I slept. I had heard it muttered in the courtyard as I braided reeds on the doorstone. And once, coming swiftly into the courtyard, I had heard the Lady say it clear as a cuckoo. "Arthur! A good thing it was we gave the sword to your Arthur."

I paused on the trail, grasping at memories like dreams. This name Arthur . . . Bear Man? . . . conjured up a Human hero, an armed giant astride a huge horse, one of whom Merlin might sing a Latin lay.

Arthur will drown both you witches.

Most likely Arthur was a common kingdom name?

Under my shirt, Otter Mellias' crystal warmed my breast.

Smiling, Otter Mellias stepped into my path.

Mellias was smaller than I, thinner, sprightlier. He wore quiet dun deerskin, invisible as our cloaks, but sunlight woke new winking lights in his braid, at his neck, wrists and ankles. I had never seen gems before, but I knew that these were gems, and I knew whose they had been.

I said coldly, "Mellias, that Human back there. What will you do with her?"

He smiled at me close-mouthed, shielding his fierce canines. Well

11

I knew that Mellias liked me. I thought I might like him, too, at the next Flowering Moon dance. I was feeling ready, maybe . . . almost . . . for my first lover.

"Niviene!" He murmured, "You are jealous of my bronze girl."

I shrugged this off. "She is the first Human to set foot here since the Romans. The Lady will not be pleased."

"The Lady is like an Old One, from before the Humans came. I respect her magic endlessly. But she is my friend. Almost like you, Niviene. So do not fear for me."

I recoiled as though from a rearing adder. "Fear! I fear for none, Mellias—least of all for you!"

"Good. You have no heart, Niviene. One of these days your power will rival the Lady's." Mellias looked past me to Elana. "What do you think, will Niviene dance with me when the moon flowers?"

Elana, behind me, must have answered him with her fingers. He laughed. "One of you girls, think of me! I think of you all the time. When you see the moon rise in flower, when you hear drum and pipe, remember me. Either one of you. Both of you." But Mellias' brown eyes clung to mine.

For the space of a haughty sigh I looked away and Mellias vanished.

I said to Elana, "Let's go home."

Lady Villa is built of earth's bones; rock. Yet not rock as it lies in earth, but what the Lady called "dressed rock." As a child I thought it must certainly have been formed by magic. I could not believe that Humans had raised it, stone by stone. But so the Lady said.

I cried, "Humans have no magic!"

"Be not so sure, Niviene. Remember, Merlin is half Human. Human druids and witches work magic. Then too, the strongest power in the world is a Human mystery of which we Fey are ignorant."

I stared up at her.

"Well. Every creature has its own mystery. But as for this villa, Humans built it as they usually build, with hands and iron tools."

Disbelieving, I looked around at the thick stone walls, the flagged floors on which I had learned to walk. "Those villagers out there in the kingdom did this with their hands?"

"Their great grandfathers did. But it was not their idea. They built it for the Romans who lived here then."

"Where are these Romans now?"

"They went away. Then the forest moved in, and the boar and the bear and the Fey. Nothing remains here now of the Romans but this villa, and the apple trees."

For many years no one had sheltered in the villa. It stood out, stark white stone against the green or dun island. Looking across the lake, neither friend nor foe could fail to see it. So the villa housed bats, owls and adders till slowly, gently, it sank back into the forest. Kind vines crawled over it. Lichens greened the harsh white stone. Apple saplings and alders crowded against its walls. And one day the Lady, heavy with child—with me!—looked across the lake and saw the villa only because she knew it was there.

Hah! The perfect birthing den! Sheltered, defensible, and nearly invisible now. She heaved herself into the nearest coracle, poled across and bore me just within the entrance.

There at the entrance a pebble picture is embedded in the floor. A graceful girl carries a basket among tall, foreign flowers. Her back is turned to us. Her light brown hair—like Elana's—flows down her green gown. Her feet are bare. Thoughtfully she touches a flower as she would touch a friend.

I was born on this picture. I learned to walk on it, and named my colors from it. I think my brother Lugh and I must be the only Fey children in the world who ever saw a picture—and such a strange picture, at that—of a foreign girl with foreign flowers. I think this picture prepared both of us for our unusual destinies.

I named the girl in the picture Dana. After "Mama," "Dana" was the first word I said. Later I asked the Lady why Dana and her flowers had no auras.

We stood together in the shadowed entry, looking down at Dana by our feet. The Lady said, "The artist who created her was Human."

"Human!" My childish ideas about Humans danced in confusion. "Most Humans do not see auras. Many Fey do not."

I stared up at the Lady. At that time—now long, long ago—she looked very much as I look now. Though she seemed tall to my young eyes, in truth she was smaller than Mellias; her grave, quiet features were delicately molded as if from brown river-clay. Her black braid swung below her hip. At home in the villa she wore graceful linen gowns that Merlin brought from afar.

Her aura swirled slowly around her, a gently sparkling silver mist like sunny, windless water. It filled the dim entry where we stood; we were as though drowned in it, as if we stood at the bottom of a deep pool. I had no idea then that my mother's aura was extraordinary. I had not yet seen the usual narrow, muddy auras that herald small minds, or minds domineered by bodies—except, of course, for wild creatures. I knew the slow, green pulse of plant auras; the flashing, vanishing brilliance of bird or fish auras; and I had glimpsed from afar the wider, steadier auras of bear and deer. But I thought then that every thinking creature—Fey or Human—would naturally walk in a broad, bright mist like the Lady, like Merlin. If Lugh's aura was orange and narrow and sometimes muddy, well, that was because he was just a young boy. He, and his aura, would surely grow.

Not to see auras would be half-blindness. How would you know what to expect of a living being? How could you walk past it, or turn your back on it? You could not know what it felt, what it might do.

The Lady laughed softly down into my upturned face. "Niviene, your aura leaps like a flame! You love to learn."

I still love to learn.

As the lone, and often lonely, girl-child of Apple Island I imagined the girl in the floor picture, Dana, and chattered to her, till she rose up off the floor, turned and showed me her homely, gentle face. She drifted with me through the villa, a secondary ghost, a thought-form I myself projected. There were other spirits there.

At dusk I might meet a bent old woman straining under burdens.

If I met her at the north end of the villa her burdens would be piles of clothes: laundry, or sewing. At the south end she would struggle with a heavy sack of peas or beans.

In the courtyard I sometimes glimpsed a merry little boy about my own age. He pulled a little wheeled cart over the paving stones, or lined up dim carved figures on the rim of the dead fountain. Once I saw him jump about in the fountain, splashing invisible water.

Unlike the exhausted old woman, the boy seemed to notice me. He would pause in his play to stare in my direction. I tried to talk to him, but the Lady warned me.

"Do not encourage ghosts, Niviene. Give them no power."

"I want to play with him!"

"You are lonely. One of these days you will go free in the forest and meet living friends."

Doubtfully, I stared up into the Lady's calm, brown face. I knew a little about this "going free in the forest." My brother had told me somewhat on his rare, secret visits.

"Why secret?" I asked him once in sunshine, beside the fountain.

"Gods, Niv, the others mustn't know! They'd get sick, laughing at me." Graphically, Lugh acted out how sick "they" would get.

"Why?"

"Look, I'm not . . . I'm supposed to . . . I'm practically grown up, Niv."

"You are not." Lugh stood a head taller than me. I had to look up to him. But I had to look up to everyone, even my ghost-friend Dana.

"You know, I guard you. I keep dragons and Humans out of the forest. And I take care of myself. I hunt and steal for me. I find my night shelter, for me. I'm grown up, Niv."

I find my night shelter, for me. I thought of the Lady's bearskin cloak, wrapped around us both, of her warmth along my back, her arm over me, me curled into her warm body all the way.

I decided and declared, "I won't go free in the forest! Not ever."

"You'll have to," Lugh assured me.

15

"Not me."

"Everyone does. Even you."

But I decided there and then that I would always stay in Lady Villa. And in a sense, I always have.

After my birth the Lady stayed. The villa made a fine den. Sunshine poured into the protected courtyard. Not all the roofs leaked rain. You could sleep dry on a stormy night, warm in winter. And we were left entirely alone.

The Fey always keep a respectful distance, one from another. But with the Lady they kept also a fearful distance.

Humans fear us Fey and leave us very much alone. They call us "the Good Folk," though we are not good to them; and "the Fair Folk," though we are dark. They never speak our name aloud: "Fey."

In much the same way, the mainland Fey feared my mother. They called her "the Lady," never by her name, Nimway. Their fishing coracles stayed well out from the island. Only those in great need sought her healings and prophecies. Till slippery Otter Mellias raised his neighboring cabin, Apple Island belonged strictly to her, Lugh and me. Apple Island and Lady Villa trapped us and transformed us into a unit resembling a Human family, in which a growing child would grow a feeling heart.

The Lady's friend Merlin, a half-Human mage, was almost a part of this "family." He would come and stay, sometimes for a season, and then return to the outside kingdom.

Because he was half Human, Merlin had once had a family. He had even known his Fey father. I thought this stranger than his magic. From birth I had watched the Lady raise wind and call wild creatures, but I knew nothing of my father, or any other relative.

Merlin once whittled me a small whistle shaped like a thrush. Whittling, he told me, "My mother was Human. My father was Fey."

I stared from the wooden thrush to his intent face. The Human mother I could imagine: shared bed-cloak, warm breasts—a giant version of my own mother. But the Fey father . . .

So Merlin had been a child, like me?

At that time his hair and Human-style beard were brown, his thin shoulders straight. The slim white fingers that whittled my thrush were not of different lengths, like the Lady's, or Lugh's. Four of them were of one length, like mine. And they were all equally dexterous. All my young life I had watched those fingers shape oak cakes, scale fish or sweep across harp strings. I loved Merlin's pale hands, and sometimes I flexed my own brown, even-lengthed fingers and tried tricks with them; but mine were less talented, stiffer, than Merlin's.

I asked him, "Were you like me, Merlin?"

He glanced a smile at me across the thrush-shaped whistle. "Yes, and no. I was small. I lived with my mother, and people left us alone. But . . ." He paused to study the whistle, over, around and under.

"But what, Merlin?"

"I was Human, and I had power."

I understood. Small Merlin had magical talent. He dreamed true and talked with ghosts, as I could not talk with the merry little boy in the courtyard.

I said, "I see ghosts."

"You have power, too. Very certainly, you have power, and will have more."

"Will I grow up magic?"

"I see you growing up powerful. You are Nimway's daughter, after all."

"I wish I knew my father."

"You Fey do not need fathers, Niv."

"How did you know your father?"

"We used to run off to the woods to see him. Always near midsummer time, when the Goddess smiles and Humans forget to scowl." Merlin handed me the finished whistle. "What does this wood tell your hands?"

My small hands cradled the thrush-whistle. "It says, *Rain* . . ." I pressed it to my cheek. "It loves rain, Merlin, and sun . . . but something's been eating it. It doesn't feel good."

17

"That's why I cut that branch out."

"But it's still alive."

"Not for long. See, you can watch the aura fade."

In truth, the faint green aura faded a bit farther ..tched.

A shadow moved over my head. I felt the Lady's vi. .t presence behind me. Merlin said to her, "Small Niviene has power."

She murmured, "Naturally. She, at least, is mine."

After this, Merlin and the Lady trained me daily. Mage children learn the warts-off spell first of all, because it works so easily. I didn't know what warts were, but I learned the spell; and when Lugh next paddled home across the lake, amazingly, he had warts, and I cured them myself.

I learned to scry, first in water, then in fire. Soon I could scry all of Apple Island in a bowl of water: where basket reeds were thickest; how ripe were the beechnuts; in what bramble thicket a rabbit hid. I learned to cast a veil of silver mist around myself to keep wolf or bear at a distance. I learned to rub and warm my palms and set kindling on fire. ("You set a fire only in a fireplace," the Lady reminded me often. Even Fey children often play with fire.)

I learned, also, that Lugh could do none of these things. "Not even warts?"

"Not even warts, Niv. I've just got no magic."

Lugh had other gifts, Human-type gifts of body, heart and energy. When he found me playing idly with an adder friend, he hurled a stone and killed it. No talk. No questions. Just action.

I looked up, surprised, slowly angering. "Why?"

"Don't you know these are poisonous?" He held the still-writhing corpse by its tail-tip. "Gods, he's as long as my arm! You don't play with these fellows, Niv."

"I do." I knew how to get along with them.

"Not any more. I'll tell."

"Hah! Go ahead. Tell. The Lady doesn't mind."

But Merlin did. "That's called tempting the Gods. A good thing it is that you can deal with adders and do not fear them. But there is no need to court them."

Merlin leaned and took my small face in gentle hands. "You are here in the world for some reason, Niviene. Use your power and knowledge to protect yourself, not to take foolish risks."

I growled, "I'll give Lugh warts for telling on me!"

Merlin's smile smoothed my threat away. "Be glad that you, alone among the Fey, have a brother who loves you."

❧

Humans think all Fey are small folk. That used to be true, back before Fey and Human blood mixed—so said the Lady. Now, we Fey are still small by Human standards, but not as small as Humans think. I believe it is the Children's Guard that keeps this myth alive.

A Human daring an edge of forest at dusk or dawn may glimpse a small, charcoal-painted face; a small hand may threaten with a poisoned dart. Before the Human's startled eyes, face and hand vanish in the swirl of an invisible cloak. The Human stands staring, hair stiff on head, neck, arms and legs.

If he continues to stare, he may get a poisoned dart in the throat. That ends that story. If he retreats swiftly, he may tell the story at his home fire, or in the village tavern. "Little, it was," he may whisper, glancing about him, still fearful. "No bigger than my young Tommy, mark me." And some wiser man informs him, "That's but natural. Don't you know, all of them Good Folk are little."

(My own height is quite usual among the Fey. For years now I have traveled the Human kingdom disguised as a Human boy, maybe twelve years old. Only here and there, now and then, an innkeeper or shepherd has crossed cautious fingers behind his back.)

I met Elana in the Children's Guard. She drew me from the first, maybe because she reminded me of Dana with her coarse, red-brown hair and surprisingly solid build. Maybe it was simply fear that drew us together. We were "free in the forest" for the first time together, and quite frightened, though Lugh showed and taught us much. By then, he was a Guard Leader, the only sort of leader most Fey ever acknowledge in their lives.

Elana asked me, "Why is Lugh so kind to you, Niviene?"

Easily, carelessly, I told her, "He is my brother."

"What? He is your what?"

"We have the same mother."

"Oh? How do you know?"

"We all live together. We are . . . we are . . ."

"Very good friends?"

"That, and more." I could not explain it in words.

But Elana understood. Something in her nature understood and responded, though she had never heard Merlin's stories, and knew nothing of Human-type relationships.

"Listen," Elana said later. "I want to be your brother, too."

"You can't be that."

"I know I don't have the same mother. But we could pretend."

"Oh, yes!" The idea brightened my heart. "But you still can't be my brother. You have to be my . . ." I remembered Merlin's word. "Sister. That's what you'll be. You be my sister, and I'll be yours."

Under cover of night, the Guard raided nearby villages. Humans see poorly at night, and we slipped among granaries and byres like shadows. Elana and I went together, each toting a sack as big as herself.

When we found bread, cheese or cloth on a doorstone we left that hut alone, then and for a while after. Lurking in dusk I have heard a woman tell her child, "Go put this oatcake out for the Good Folk." Her man, gobbling soup within, knew nothing of it. He would have called it waste of a good oatcake. But the wife knew that a bare doorstone meant real waste.

Finding no offerings, we Good Folk laughed open-mouthed, showing off our dagger teeth, and robbed the hut.

We snaked our ways into dark, fetid hut or sweet-smelling granary and filled our sacks. We stole into the byre and milked the goat. Close by many a sleeping family we tiptoed, watching them toss and turn together, kick and push and yank at their bedclothes. We watched infants nurse at sleeping mothers' breasts.

Rarely, a Fey might steal a sleeping infant from his mother's bed. It was almost as easy as stealing a loaf of bread, so said the Lady. Elana and I never did that, for we never had a customer waiting back in the forest. Fey mothers whose babies had died bartered for these babies; or Fey women unblessed by the Goddess, who wished to sacrifice to Her nonetheless by raising a child, though they could bear none.

At times I sensed a presence that hovered in the close, heavy air of these Human dens. But I would live long and travel far before I understood that presence, the Human mystery of which the Lady had told me, of which we Fey are ignorant.

Once an ancient man sat up and looked at me. As he moved his aura flared, a low dull flame in the dark. Among us Fey such a decrepit oldster would by now have wandered away to give his bones back to the Goddess. But Human families keep their old ones close, and their sick ones, and sometimes even deformed children.

I stood still as a cornshock, leaning forward, one hand out-stretched to snatch the spread cloak off his feet. I slowed my breathing. Across the hut, Elana stuffed bread and cheese into her sack. She did not know the old one was awake, and I could not signal her.

The ancient swung stringy legs off the pallet. I guessed he was making for the piss pot, and we would collide. I could not tell whether he saw me. Human eyes are weak in the dark, and many oldsters cannot see well even by daylight.

He gathered himself to rise, and looked up into my face. A long moment he sat, eyes meeting mine. Then he folded his hands, bowed his head, and watched me from under lowered brows.

He saw me. He saw me, but he would do nothing. He would not yell and wake the sleepers, or scramble up and grab me, or even hold onto his cloak. He thought I could point at him, intone a word, and turn him into a toad.

Joyous power surged through me. I drew the dark cloak up, away, and over me. For him, I vanished into darkness. Then I touched Elana's shoulder. We tiptoed out the door.

We ran lightly away. That is, I ran lightly. Elana bounded like a fat hare, heels thumping earth. Safe in the shadow of the Fey forest, we burst out laughing.

Later we murmured together under the old man's smelly bed-cloak about boys, men and sex. We had to murmur. We could not sign in the dark. I said, "I don't want to."

"You mean, you aren't ready."

"What about you?"

"Hshh!" groaned a companion across the small fire. "Are you two going to talk all night?"

"I'm ready!" Elana whispered.

"But you don't."

"It's . . . hard to explain."

"Hushshshshs!" from across the fire.

"Try. Explain."

Elana squirmed further under the cloak and I followed. It smelled, down there, of Human and age, dust, sweat, meat, soup, sickness. Someone had vomited on this cloak, long ago. Elana's breath on my cheek smelled of thyme and trout. Her whispered words tickled first my ear, then my thought.

"It's . . . There is one."

"One what?"

"One man, silly. Or boy, rather."

"So why don't you?"

"See, there's only one. One only. And he doesn't want me."

"That's funny," I giggled.

Across the fire our sleepless companion sighed, gathered up his cloak and wandered off in search of peace.

"It is not funny! It feels bad. In here." Elana took my fingers and pressed them where her heart beat, under her soft-sprouting breast.

Repentant, I kissed her cheek. "Why don't you try someone else, then? At the next Flowering Moon dance. There's lots of boys, Elana."

"Not for me. There's only one for me." Elana wept.

I lay astonished, feeling her heart beat under my fingers, feeling her tears warm on my face. I remembered something.

"Elana, my mother has a friend called Merlin."

"The mage. I know."

"He used to sing Human songs to us—old stories about heroes and princesses."

"So?"

"Elana, in those stories the Humans used to feel like you do."

Elana stiffened. "They did?"

"Yes. There would be only one for them, and if they couldn't have that one they would go meet a dragon or something . . . they didn't want to live."

"I thought . . . I thought it was just me!" The warm tears still flowed, but the beating heart quieted like a bird that you hold still in the dark between your palms.

"No, it's something Humans feel. But most times those Humans were bewitched."

"Bewitched!"

"They had a spell on them. That's why they felt that way."

"Gods!"

"Maybe you are bewitched."

"How do you get over being bewitched?"

"I don't know. In the stories, they never do." I dried Elana's closing eyes with a cloak-corner.

"So what do they do, in the stories?"

"Either they meet and love, or they let a dragon eat them. Something like that."

"Hah! I've never seen a dragon, have you?"

"Elana, let's sleep now."

"In this stink?"

Half-laughing now, we wiggled our heads out from under the cloak and gasped clean night air.

Merlin said, "I dreamt a summer storm."

"Not serious," the Lady said.

"Not serious for Arthur. As you well know, I take no store in the woman."

They knew about Mellias' captive, and about her Arthur. They knelt together at the courtyard fireplace where Lugh's trout cooked on the hot stones. Lugh crouched with them; and Elana and I drifted near in our invisible cloaks, drawn by the hot fish smell.

"You would not mind," the Lady asked, "if her body fed our starved apple trees?"

Her braid was still midnight black. Merlin's bush of hair and beard had gone grey. They leaned together like an aged pair of geese, like a long-married Human couple.

"I would not mind," Merlin said. "But you might."

"Why should I mind?"

"You don't expect Arthur to sit still and accept the theft of his wife?"

"Why should he not? You have told me there is little love there."

Merlin sighed. "This is not a matter of love, Nimway. It is a matter of pride."

"Pride? . . . Oh. Pride."

"You understand."

"I am trying."

"Arthur may well gather his iron-armed, mounted companions and charge into your forest. No children's poisoned darts would stop that charge."

"What harm could they do? Those awkward giants armed like beetles could not catch a one of us!"

"Your forest would be known, Nimway. No longer enchanted and forbidden." Thoughtfully, Merlin stroked his grey beard. "All this while I have magicked for Arthur to save your forest from Saxon invasion. Now it seems Arthur may invade it himself."

The Lady smiled, close-mouthed. "You magicked for Arthur himself, Merlin. The Human part of you has always loved Arthur."

"That is true." Merlin admitted it gravely. "You may smile. You did not carry the newborn child through the storm in your cloak."

"Not that child, no."

"You did not watch him grow, and keep the secret. And you are not Human."

"Thank all Gods!"

"There may be two ways to look at that matter too, Nimway. Every story has at least two sides." Merlin gazed deeply at the Lady a moment, then swung away to pace. "For Arthur's sake I would forget the woman. Her stars and his are wrong together. I told him as much before the marriage."

"That must have been the only time he disregarded you."

"It was. That time, Human politics outweighed reason. But for your sake, Nimway, for the sake of the Fey, she must go home, safely and soon."

Forgotten Lugh squawked, "But she can't simply walk out of here!"

His voice broke as he made this astonishing, clear statement—as though he knew whereof he spoke—in front of the wise Lady and Mage Merlin.

He blushed from his dark hairline down to the neck of his tunic. (Lugh was the only Fey I ever knew who was fair enough to blush. Well, there was Elana, but I suspected her of Human blood anyway.)

Merlin and the Lady stared at Lugh. A tension tingled the air.

He glanced from one to the other and back, lowered his lustrous dark eyes and tossed his hair forward like a shield. He leaned to spear a trout with a stick. Wresting it into his bark bowl, he explained gruffly, "You know I study the kingdom and know somewhat what goes on there."

The Lady trilled a low, light laugh, as a bird may call after thunder. "In truth," she murmured, "I wish you studied less and knew less!"

25

Merlin's bent brows relaxed. He said, "Knowledge is always good, Nimway. What do you know, young Lugh, that we have not considered?"

So gently had Lugh and I been raised, so safe did we feel in Lady Villa—our home—that Lugh straightway raised his head, brushed his hair back with his hand, and began to speak in his new, manly tones, with no break in his voice.

He spoke of Human mysteries: marriage, law, war, Saxons, alliances. Merlin and the Lady exchanged amused glances.

He spoke then of Gwenevere—the woman we found under the apple tree—of her famous beauty (so Humans accounted her beautiful, as I did myself!) and of her well-known headstrong nature. (Headstrong? Not just now.)

Merlin said gently, "All this we know, Lugh."

"But you must then realize, Sir . . . True it is that she must go home! But she cannot walk away like a village girl some Fey fool has ravished and let go!"

Merlin said, "You may not believe this, but queens can be bewitched like peasants."

"Oh, I know!" Lugh cried. He saw now that he was not being seriously consulted, but played with. He blushed again, this time from anger. "Like the girl I mentioned just now, she can walk out of here and speak of trees that held her prisoner, and deer that turned into lovers, and how days passed like moments. And our forest will be all the safer because she walked out of it."

Merlin smiled. "So, what are you saying?"

"I'm saying . . . well, for one thing, she cannot leave here in the rags she is wearing."

The Lady asked softly, "How do you know what she is wearing, Lugh?"

Lugh flung down his bowl, fish and all, and stamped on it. The fish being sizzling hot, he then hopped about awhile with no semblance of dignity. No one smiled. Courteously, we all waited for his answer.

"Very well!" he gasped finally. "Very well! I have seen her. She's been here some days now."

Merlin asked, "Have you played with her?"

"They . . . they didn't give me a turn."

"That is well," Merlin said slowly. "That is very well. Yes, you are right. Gwenevere must be better dressed."

"And she cannot walk alone!"

"Why not?"

"Gods, she cannot walk at all! She must ride away on a palfrey, led by a . . ."

"A trusted knight."

"Yes."

Merlin glanced at the Lady. She looked up into the shining sky, and then away from us. Face turned away from us, she shrugged.

Merlin said, "Lugh. You used to play Tournament with the village boys, did you not."

"I . . . yes." Lugh's voice cracked on the word. Merlin had taken him by surprise.

"You can handle a horse."

"Why, yes. I mean, I suppose so."

"You know how to handle arms. Not in combat, but so you won't stumble over them."

"Oh, yes. I can handle arms!" Lugh's stormy face began to clear.

"You would no doubt enjoy a journey into the kingdom."

Lugh swallowed, choked, coughed. "Anything I can do! . . . Any way I can serve!"

"Fear not," Merlin soothed him, unnecessarily. "I will go with you."

Joy burst like fire out of Lugh. His reddish aura, which had been invisible in the strong light, now swept over and around him like a cloud. His face shone like the sun, his eyes gleamed like stars.

Erect as an angry serpent the Lady turned and glided away from us. Her long gown swished on the paving stones, a sound like coming rain.

⊷⊶

Elana said, "Lugh is going!"

I replied, "He has always wanted to."

We lay close together on soft moss under Counsel Oak. A spring breeze rustled Counsel's leaves. Thrush and warbler talked among the leaves, and cuckoos argued across the island.

Elana said, "But where? But why?"

Elana had never heard Merlin's kingdom songs. The other day she had looked for the first time on Dana in the villa entrance, and the foreign fish leaping on the wall; she had gazed at them blankly, with mindless eyes. Elana had no conception of a world beyond our forest. She saw Lugh wandering off into the open, terrifying distance of the kingdom into . . . nothing.

The thought of trying to explain numbed my tongue. I shrugged and repeated, "Always he has wanted to go out there. Since we were little. Merlin used to say he would outgrow it—like a tic, you know."

Cross-legged by the courtyard fire the Lady held my tiny form in her lap, and I felt the strong, steady shake of her head above me: No.

Merlin slapped dough on hot stones. The rich smell of oatcake drifted about us. Over my head the Lady's sorrow-laden voice said, "My son will grow up and go. It is in his blood. Can you stop a swan from swimming?"

This sad prophecy stayed with me. Throughout childhood I would dream this moment, and wonder, waking, what it meant. What sorrow weighed my mother's voice?

Now Elana moaned, "But what is there to go to, out there? What does he want?"

I wondered at her misery. Why should Elana mind if Lugh dressed up like a young knight, climbed on top of a horse and rode kingdom-way? What was it to her? "There's another world," I told her patiently, "beyond this one where we live."

It was, by Merlin's accounts, a strange and dangerous world. Here, when you see a snowstorm coming, you build a shelter. When

28

wolves approach, you climb a tree. The simple dangers of our own world are simply met. But out in the giant's kingdom one might not see danger approach. One might break some rule, unknowingly; one might offer insult, innocently; and we Fey knew only one defense—to shrink, hide, disappear. You could hardly do that in the open fields of the kingdom.

Anxiety brushed my heart with thorny fingers. Lugh, my brother, was going out there for no very good reason, out where he could barely understand the language, and probably knew less of the rules than he thought. He was going openly, perfectly visible, mounted on a tall horse, weighed down with armor and spear.

He was going where he had always wanted to go. I was not going. What was it to me? My almost-Human heart stirred restlessly.

Elana said, "At least the Otter is going with him!"

"What?" I sat up at that. "Otter Mellias? Why in the name of all Gods is *he* going?"

"He will be Lugh's . . . servant? Squire? I heard words like those."

"But . . . Mellias knows no more of the kingdom than you do! How can he manage out there?"

Elana lay still, gazing up into Counsel's sunny leaves. Her aura flickered green against green moss and the green-lichened trunk. Before, it had licked like hungry flame. Now it calmed, as she thought of Lugh somehow protected by Mellias.

"He will be . . . deaf? Unable to hear. Thus, he will not have to speak."

"Are there deaf Humans?"

"Merlin says so."

"I didn't know that. When did you hear this?"

"Last night. While you slept."

I sat stiffly in sunshine and bird song, thinking of small, brown Mellias visible in the kingdom. Strange prickles of anxiety raked my heart. "But why?"

"You'll have to ask him." Elana turned her eyes to me. Like Lugh's, they were grey, heavy-lashed, thoughtful and hinted at hidden depths. "What is it to you, Niv?"

"By the Gods, I cannot say!"

Elana scrutinized me. "You like Mellias."

"I . . . yes. I like him." I had been thinking of dancing with him at the Flowering Moon, now days away.

"Niv," Elana said, "listen to Counsel's leaves."

I listened. I heard the wind in the leaves become voices, far away, indistinct. Bird calls drowned their words. "I can't hear, Elana."

"Maybe Merlin will prophesy. They won't send those two out there without a prophecy!"

"Maybe the Lady will read her crystal . . ."

So we consoled each other in the sunshine, on soft moss, at the massive foot of Counsel Oak.

⁓❧⁓

Merlin's even-lengthened fingers swept the strings of the small harp he called Enchanter.

He sat cross-legged away from the fire, on the edge of the dark, and as his fingers woke the magic strings they sighed like the leaves of Counsel Oak. I shivered a little, and my eyelids sank, that I might better see bright dreams.

I jerked myself awake. On this night I wanted to see and observe and remember, not to be magicked by some wild Human story.

Our feast-fire barely glowed in the stone fireplace. Elana and Lugh sat leaning together, staring into the coals. Mellias dozed, stretched out on his back, one foot balanced on one raised knee.

Beside him his captive Gwen crouched, half awake. Through the tatters of the blue gown her slim body shone, moon-white. When the thought occurred she pulled her long, loose hair over her breasts, only to let it go a moment later. Her vague eyes passed over Merlin—whom she knew—as though over a stranger, and lingered on Lugh.

Eyes bright, sitting up squirrel-straight, the Lady sent me a barely visible smile and raised her fingers to sign, *You grip your wits about you!*

I smiled back. We understood each other.

Under Merlin's fingers the harp Enchanter leaf-rustled, water-rippled, wind-sang; and Merlin began a story.

"If of love and death you'd hear,
If gladly you would shed a tear
For grief long past and lovers dead,
For helpless guilt and magicked dread,
Come listen to my tale of woe
That like an arrow shot from bow
Will pierce your heart
In tend'rest part."

Then, in quick prose: "Here comes my hero, Sir Tristam, over the sea—which is a very large lake—in his ship, which is a very large coracle. And Sir Tristam himself is a very large hero, a Human, what we call a giant; and the maiden who comes to greet him, dark hair blowing, bright gown flowing, the Princess Yseult, is a giantess like Gwen."

I looked at Gwen and imagined Yseult more clearly than ever before—though of course Yseult was richly clad and in her right mind. It was not Gwen's fault that she crouched near-naked among enemies. She might well be the heroine of a great Latin song, for she was lovely, fairer to see than . . . than the Lady, whose beauty was famed in the forest. And beauty makes a Human heroine, I have noticed. Wit, gift and power are of far less account. In truth, Human women of mind or magic are usually evil-doers in Human tales.

The story progressed. Sir Tristam, a knight such as Lugh so admired, had come to seek Yseult—not to lie with her, strangely, but to take her back home so his uncle, King Mark, could lie with her. (This part of the tale is impossible to explain to Fey, and Merlin did not try. He merely remarked that the Human way of life demanded some odd activities.) Yseult agreed to go lie with King Mark, sight unseen. And her mother, one of those suspect women of mind and magic, gave her a love potion to share with King Mark, so they two would surely love each other.

Now Merlin's harp music rolled like the sea that Tristam and Yseult sailed together. They feasted under the tilting stars and Yseult's maid brought them a drink to share; by bitter ill fortune, that drink was the mother's love potion.

Now, Yseult's mother knew her magic spells! As soon as Tristam and Yseult drank that potion they fell deeply, hopelessly, forever in love. They were bewitched (as I thought Elana must be bewitched. So foolish, so Human was she about the only one she loved, Elana reminded me powerfully of this story. Here I found the only possible explanation of her condition.).

So Tristam and Yseult loved where, by Human custom and thought, they must not love. They desired only each other, and King Mark and his kingdom could sink into the underworld for all they cared. Here began much grief and torment for Mark, and for his kingdom, and for the bewitched lovers.

Merlin's harp music sank away now from roar to murmur, from water-ripple to leaf-rustle.

Elana leaned her head on Lugh's shoulder, wet-eyed and dreamy. One plump, white hand had captured one of his.

Lugh looked over Elana's head at Gwen.

Gwen looked at Lugh as though she saw him through her Mushroom fog.

And Merlin struck the harp, Enchanter, one final, deep chord that echoed even in my heart.

⚜

Bright under the rising sun, East River swirled under our two coracles. Flocks of ducks and swans rose on thundering wings as we bore down on them. They flew over us and settled in our wake.

Gwen, Mellias and I rode in one coracle, Lugh and Elana in the other. Elana and I held the poles athwart the rims. Rushing downstream, we had no need to pole.

Between gleaming sun and glinting water I saw my friends, birds, the trees leaning over the banks, as solid figures only, catching and reflecting sunlight as Merlin tells me the moon does, itself lightless. But I could feel the auras I could not see. From Gwen in my boat to Lugh in Elana's stretched a taut line of power. Steadily, Lugh watched Gwen; and Elana's furious grey gaze should have bored a hole in the back of his head. When their coracle bumped ours I felt Elana's rage like a whirlpool around both coracles.

Gwen sat silent, staring at passing trees. Her focusing eyes showed that the Mushroom was wearing off. At East Edge she should be able to mount the palfrey Merlin had found for her, a thing she must do every day in her kingdom life. She might even remember some of what she saw now swiftly glide past: close, dark trees, flying ducks, a tree house overhanging water, small dark children splashing.

Mellias groomed himself like a happy otter. He loosened his braid and did it up, brushed leaves from his tunic, checked and rechecked his bulging pouches. Mellias was going far.

"But why, Mellias?" I had asked him sadly.

"You surprise me, Niviene! Have you never wanted to see the world?"

"Why, no." The thought had never brushed my mind.

"And you hearing Merlin's stories when you were small! And seeing pictures!"

"I was quite content with stories and pictures, Mellias. I still am."

"Never mind, Sweet. I'll be back before the moon flowers twice."

"I do not think so." I had a gloomy vision of vast distance, suspended time.

"I'll dance with you yet for the Flowering Moon, Niviene. That thought will bring me back!"

"They say you are going as Lugh's . . . servant."

"Whatever that is, yes."

"It is not a noble role, Mellias. And I hope you can handle horses."

"What?"

"You will be on or near horses the entire time."

"Ah? In truth? I had some idea about a ship, you know, as in the story. A very large coracle on a very large river."

"Horses."

"Ah. Mhm." For the first time, Mellias sounded doubtful. But then Lugh came to us shining, big with excitement as a woman with child; and they trotted away together, merrily finger-talking.

I marveled at this yen for adventure shared by males as different as Mellias and my brother. Nothing, I thought, would ever draw me away from the safe shadows of our forest.

East River widened and slowed. Trees along the banks thinned out, patches of sunrise light speckled the forest floor. I glanced over at Elana and nodded.

She sat in a thundercloud of her own making. I gasped, my heart lurched, at sight of her miserable fury.

But she saw my nod and raised her pole as I raised mine. Together we thrust poles down through clear water and weeds into firm bottom. Together we turned the coracles into shore. Cautiously we crept around the next bend, poling through rustling reeds, invisible among them; for now we were at the eastern edge of the forest, which we had guarded as children—actually on the edge of the Human kingdom.

I stood up to look over the swaying reeds and the bank and saw again the kingdom stretch out before me. (I had not expected to see this sight so soon again. I still expected a quiet, hidden life on Apple Island, or in the secret depths of our forest, far and safe from this expanse of sky and treeless earth, and the confused, driven folk who worked in it.)

Pasture bordered the forest, grazing for great flocks of sheep and goats and small herds of half-wild ponies. Beyond, smoke from three thatched villages smudged the sunrise. In their midst reared Midsummer Tor, a small cone-shaped hill where Elana and I had danced with Humans one midsummer night. (To this day I never glimpse that tor but I remember.) Between us and the tor, bowed men and strained oxen were plowing fields.

34

Skylarks dived and sang in the brightening sky. The calls of sheep and cattle came to us in the reeds, and smells of dung and smoke and another, close, hot animal smell I could not place. And all this flat, foreign distance lay perfectly open before us, screened by an occasional great shade tree and a few hedgerows where a rabbit might vanish, but not a Fey. The awful vista caught my breath and stilled my heart, as it always had.

We climbed out of the coracles and splashed to shore. Elana and I dragged in the coracles. Only Gwen sat still, misty-eyed, white hands folded in lap.

Lugh splashed to her. He lifted her out of the coracle, this great, powerful boy; he carried her in his arms and set her ragged-slippered feet on the bank and steadied her, his muscled arm tight about her waist.

This surprised me, but I forgot it as Merlin appeared beside us, the Lady at his elbow. They had horses waiting in the forest shadows. (That was the source of the baffling animal smell.) They had a sack of clothing, light armor for Lugh, a gown and cloak for Gwen. Merlin would go as he was, and Lugh's deaf servant needed no finery.

The Lady gave the rolled-up gown and cloak to Gwen, who cradled them as she might cradle a baby.

"Dress yourself," the Lady told her.

Gwen stood, swaying, hugging the bundle.

"You can dress yourself." The Lady rose tiptoe to peer up into Gwen's eyes. "Mushroom's wearing off . . . ah. I know." She turned to us. "She wants to dress hidden."

Buckling his new cuirass, Lugh snorted. "In truth! Elana, take her into that thicket and help her."

"What!" Elana stiffened. "What?"

"Help Gwen dress."

"Is she a baby?"

"She's a Roman lady, Elana. She's a Queen." Lugh seemed to think those words would silence all argument.

I stood there amazed. Lugh did not see auras. Obviously he did

35

not see the storm cloud in which Elana stood. But could he not feel her rage and grief, as even Human haymakers feel a coming storm? Lugh went on struggling with the unfamiliar buckles, and Mellias played with the new weapons, hefting and testing. Neither seemed to notice anything unusual about Elana.

Myself, I reacted and sneaked the knife from her belt. Myself, I took Gwen's large, freckled fingers in my small, brown hand and led her away.

In a thicket well known to Elana and me I took Elana's knife and slit Gwen's rags off her. Naked, she swayed like a gold-freckled birch. She shuddered in the sudden chill, and her grey eyes brightened a bit.

I considered her. Unwillingly I called, "Elana! We need a comb here."

Glowering, Elana materialized beside me and handed me a bone comb. I offered it to Gwen, but she only stared at it. So myself, I went to work on her long bright hair.

Combing, I said, "Elana. You know why Gwen is going home safely to her man. And you know why Lugh is going with her."

"And you know, Niviene, that Lugh will never come back."

My combing hand paused. Gwen stood placid as a well-trained horse.

Darkness whipped around Elana like a cloak. She clapped hand to where her knife should have hung and froze, astonished.

"Elana," I asked quietly, "why do you give Lugh such power to hurt you?"

Elana opened her mouth, but no words came out. She raised her fingers to answer me.

Lugh is the one. The only one.

I should have know that.

I must have know that.

I asked nothing more of Elana. Myself, I braided Gwen's amazing, glinting hair into one long plait and bound it with her own ribbon from my pouch. Myself, I took the bundled blue gown from her arms, rose tiptoe and wrestled it over her head. While she pushed her arms into the sleeves I swung the brown cloak over her shoulders. There she stood combed and dressed, once more lovely to me as a goddess. (I had no notion how modest her outfit was. She should have worn a tunic and overgown, gathered with a jeweled girdle. A knife should have stood in the girdle, and keys on a gold chain, and her slippers should have been clean; and a light veil would have done no harm.)

I said, "Come, Gwen," and tugged at her fingers and led her away past Elana, out to the others.

Lugh looked up at her from his new sword and stood thunderstruck.

Sun glinted off his cuirass and helmet. (Impossible now for Lugh to vanish in a thicket!) He looked like any very young knight who might ride past the forest edge, glancing uneasily into the shadows. Elana and I used to toss cones from treetops at such and laugh to see them touch new spurs to horse.

Lugh recovered from the stunning effect of Gwen's beauty. Or maybe he was inspired to impress her. He turned to his new servant and commanded grandly, "Mell. Fetch the horses."

Mellias' mouth hung open as he contemplated Gwen in her modest glory. Now he turned startled eyes to Lugh, and paled.

"Go on."

Mellias made no move.

"You've handled horses, haven't you?"

"Ah. Not . . . lately."

"Very well. I'll show you." Distinctly swaggering, Lugh led Mellias into the shade.

(From the thicket behind us, Elana and I used to watch Lugh ride with the village boys. They would ride at each other on ponies, donkeys or their brothers, and hit each other real blows with real sticks. They called this incredibly stupid game Tournament. The idea was to knock as many others off their mounts as you could before you were knocked off yours.

Lugh played often with Human boys. They fascinated him, as did all things Human. He would come at them from the east, circling round, so they thought he was Human, like them, only from some farther village they did not know. Much to the Lady's disgust he had never let his teeth be filed, so he could laugh open-mouthed, and they saw only ragged, slimy teeth like their own. Learning their rough, wolf-cub games, he also learned their language and ways.)

Horses held no terror for Lugh. He marched right up to those waiting in the shade. "You can't be cautious with them," he told Mellias. "You walk up calmly, like this—"

But the horses smelled Fey. They trembled, neighed, and strained on their leads.

Merlin stroked his beard. The Lady smiled close-mouthed and leaned against an ash tree. This might take a while.

Mellias had never played Tournament. The heavy horse smell alarmed him as much as his Fey smell alarmed the horses. Mellias and the horses proceeded to circle and dodge, tangle leads, snort and kick. Almost, I heard the laughter of Guard children watching from the tree tops.

Lugh lost patience. He tramped into the dance, picked Mellias up and added him like a sack to the burden of the old pack horse, the only animal to hang his head quietly throughout the confusion. "All right. I'll lead you on a trace for today. But you'll have to learn horses to be my squire!"

Mellias shut his eyes.

Himself, Lugh led the string of horses out into the sun. Himself, he cupped his hands and helped Gwen mount the small, moon-white palfrey they had brought for her. She swung from his hands astride the horse and pulled her loose gown down, and for the first time she seemed fully aware of what she was doing.

Then Lugh cupped his hands for Merlin. The mage smiled in his beard, stepped up into Lugh's hands and thence onto a small, grey horse.

"See, Mell," said Lugh, "that's what you're supposed to do for me." But Mellias' eyes stayed shut.

Lugh clapped dust from his hands and vaulted onto a big black charger. Two horses yet unsaddled were meant for the "men at arms" who would join the band at the first "inn." Lugh was ready to hurry away, heels poised to kick, when the Lady hurried to stand at his knee.

Her back was turned to me. She spoke to Lugh with her fingers, hidden from me. So I have never known what she said to him.

I do know that Lugh had no notion at that time that he would not come back. He thought only that he was going on a wonderful adventure, free in the world, as a child goes free in the forest. Doubtless he thought he would return, as he had returned from the Children's Guard to Avalon. Maybe he thought this day of return would come soon, even as Mellias thought he would dance with me at the next Flowering Moon.

So he had little to say to the Lady. Over her head I saw him sign. *Watch us in your crystal. Weave us a spell.* Then his aura flamed into the sun and swept around his band, gathering them up as his hands gathered the charger's reins. The horses lifted their heads, blew, and stepped out.

First Lugh rode away through the flocks of sheep that dotted the pastures. His servant Mell followed on a lead, bouncing like the sacks at his belt. Gwen swayed on the white palfrey, newly expert and graceful. And Merlin, hunched under his homespun cloak, brought up the rear. They rode far and farther away from us, small and smaller, out into the kingdom.

A flock of sheep parted before them, separated lambs bawling for their mothers. They rode past the men plowing with oxen, who paused to stare. They passed under Midsummer Tor. Between us and them, skylarks climbed and soared and sang.

The three of us stood quietly, watching them dwindle out of sight. Dark energy throbbed from the Lady. She knew. She had always known.

Behind me, something screamed.

I whirled.

Tears slimed Elana's plump cheeks. From her wide-open mouth poured infantile sorrow, loss and despair. She bawled like a separated lamb.

39

Beyond the tor, the riders merged with the spring-green land.

Screeching, Elana collapsed on her knees. Her black cloud rolled over her, hiding her completely, and reached seeking, spidery arms toward me.

I ran. I rushed away from Elana and her dangerous cloud, down to the coracles in the reeds. I pushed a coracle out into the river, scrambled in and seized the pole. A moment I held the boat steady in the water, looking back.

The Lady stood half engulfed in the cloud. It reached no higher than her waist, for her brilliant energy beat it down. I dared not trust my own energy to do the same. I braced my feet, shoved the pole down and pushed away hard, upstream, against the current.

2

FLOWERING MOON

While last sunlight yet lingered the maiden moon rose. I paused, reed-thatching my night's shelter, to watch her touch the beech tops across the clearing. This glade must have been cleared for Flowering Moon dances, but it had not been used for years, and young trees were raising leafy heads out of the carpeting bluebells.

Two nights more, and the moon would flower. Drums would thrum, pipes sing. From the deepest, farthest forest shadows the Fey would gather in glades like this to dance, cavort, feast and love. Silent folk who carefully did not cross paths all month would meet that night as friends and lovers. And I had meant to meet with them, this time.

Under the beeches a moon-white figure moved. It raised a small head, twitched ears and tail, looked about. The ghost of a fallow doe?

I had seen such ghosts before. A bear haunted the pit in which he had been trapped. A wolf bounded by moonlight through snow, leaving no tracks. And this doe—

Stepped on a twig. I heard it crack.

This was a white fallow doe, warmly alive as myself. Watching her slow movements, I thought, "She has hidden a kid nearby." Softly I called to her, "Greetings, doe! We shall be friends in this clearing, you and I."

She stretched her head high and flicked an ear.

I went back to piling reeds on my shelter of bent saplings. Orioles and blackbirds sang around me. In a darker patch of forest a nightingale fluted. I thatched and thought.

Poling home to Avalon I had paused here to be alone. Maybe I had some thought that Elana's black cloud might follow me upriver to the island. Maybe I hid like a wounded animal, needing to curl down and lick my wounds. Much had happened in a very short time.

I had lost my brother. Elana said he would not return, and my bones told me she was right. Why I thought that I could not say. But I knew that the Lady had always dreaded his departure. *Can you stop a swan from swimming?* I had lost my friend Mellias almost before we made friends. I might have lost Elana. How could I ever turn to her and take her hand again, knowing her fearful weakness?

I thatched and thought, first about Lugh.

My brother Lugh had always yearned toward the Human kingdom. During his time in the Children's Guard, Lugh visited the kingdom more than he guarded against it. One midsummer night he took Elana and me out there to the bonfire on the tor.

He gave us Human-style tunics and shawls and led us out from East Edge at dusk. Like shadows we drifted hand-in-hand across pastures we knew well from our nightly forays. As we came near, the village folk streamed around us; folk from "our" village and from farther ones. We moved in this crowd like dun deer in a dun herd. As we neared the tor the drums began to beat—not soft, heart-beat drums like those the Fey use, but great, booming, thunder-drums that shook the blood in our ears.

Elana stopped. "They will suspect us!" She signed, *They will burn our bones in that fire.*

Lugh signed, *Just keep your lips closed. They'll never guess. You look perfectly Human.* (And Elana did.)

At the fire we moved straight into the forming circle. Hand-in-hand with villagers we shuffled around the rising fire.

The Human stink was overpowering. The sight of uncounted Humans together amazed me. All ages formed the circle, children barely walking, oldsters bent double, a few downright deformed persons. I had never seen such before.

These were heavy giants. Their feet lifted cautiously from the earth they knew so well. The drums beat slowly, then faster. Pipes shrilled, the pace quickened, and I saw a flame of excitement flicker around the circle.

Now the sick ones, small ones and oldsters drew back to watch. Faster we danced, hopping and jumping, higher as the fire lowered.

And then a young couple tore out of the circle, ran hand-in-hand and leaped the fire.

Amazed, I watched pairs, singles and whole strings of young folk bound like hares over the fire. Why should risk and danger enter into this joy? But such is always the Human way.

Lugh tore his hand from mine. He and Elana rushed forward and flung themselves over, hand-in-hand, clothes and hair flying among the sparks. They turned back and leaped again.

I saw their two faces uplifted, bright and wild as the Human faces around them. They might as well be Human themselves. They were both tall for Fey, and sturdy, and now I saw them crazed, ecstatic. Astonished and troubled I closed the circle, taking the hand of an old farmer on one side and a little girl on the other. My heart was beating with the drums.

Be careful, I told myself. Remember yourself and what you are, or you might jump that fire yourself!

Cautious now, I rose into spirit and looked down on the dance from a height. Safe up there, I could see the flame of joyful excitement running the circle, glowing in the dancers' faces and spurting under their feet.

Then a young fellow trailing flowery ribbons misjudged his leap and the ribbons flared. He pranced on unknowing, but dancers and bystanders ran to catch him, roll him on the ground and tear away the burning ribbons.

After this the excitement ebbed. The flame flickered more gently around the circle, and I sank down again into my body. Again I felt the calloused, sweating hands holding mine, and smelled bitter Human breath.

As the night faded the circle drifted apart. Lugh and Elana came and drew me away, and we three slipped quietly downhill. Fires, lit from the bonfire, burned below in three villages. All the way down we stumbled on couples helping the God and Goddess unite, too eager even to seek cover.

Now, placing my last reed thatch, I thought, Elana should have tumbled Lugh that night. She had had other chances since then: Flowering Moons, "accidental" meetings; she could have enticed Lugh at the villa, or in any thicket, for that matter. But I was quite sure she never had. I thought if Elana had lain with Lugh, she could have sent him away dry-eyed.

Daylight gone, I gathered sticks and leaves in a small stone circle and breathed energy into my palms. Cross-legged by the tinder I flexed my hands, cupped them, drew them apart and together, watched aura flash from palm to palm. Back then, my aura was the strong, steady green of youth and growth. It has changed color several times since then. Now it is blue-edged silver.

When I was ready I laid hands to tinder, and a small, yellow flame licked up. Even back then at the beginning of my power I scried in fire as my mother scried in crystal. I often saw coming events in flame, or waking dreams that shed new light on the past. This time I sought understanding of the recent past, especially of Elana's astounding passion. I sought guidance. How should I treat Elana so as not to catch her weakness like a fever? How should I deal with the loss of my brother? I had not known I would miss him as I already did! And, at the coming Flowering Moon, should I couple for the first time? Or should I wait yet again for another Moon?

I had made my quiet camp here by the Fey river to scry and think by myself, without the Lady looking thoughtfully over my shoulder. I leaned and looked into the flame as I might look into a reflecting pool; and in this fire-pool I saw a face reflected. Not the Lady, but a child looked down over my shoulder from her perch in the ash tree.

Perfectly still, moving no muscle, I studied the face.

My spirit must have known all this time that I was not alone; but I, Niviene, had been too busy with thoughts and feelings to hear her whispered warning.

A young girl, maybe ten years old, watched me round-eyed. She cocked her head like a fox-cub and licked thin, hungry lips. And now I could smell her: hair and skin none too clean, recently ate meat.

I said softly, "Come down here. Let us talk."

The face in the fire widened startled eyes and disappeared. I heard her drop softly to earth and pad toward me. She stepped round the fire and faced me, small hands clasped on lean stomach, black eyes huge.

I smiled close-mouthed. "What is your name?"

"Aefa."

"Aefa, do you know me?"

Nod. "You are a mage. You live on Apple Island with the Lady."

"My name is Niviene," I told her. "The Lady is my mother."

"Your mother that birthed you?"

I nodded.

"I don't know my mother."

"I do not know my father."

"Oh," said Aefa, and tossed her head, "no one knows their father."

"That's quite true. But I would like to know, wouldn't you?"

Bathing my even-toed feet, combing my coarse hair, sometimes

45

I wondered where they both came from. And my even-lengthened fingers, were those maybe Human? Merlin had such fingers, and Merlin was half Human. So I had sometimes wondered, spying on the villagers, if they might maybe be my cousins. But I would never know.

Aefa said, "No, I don't care about my father. I would like to know my mother. But Lady, I wondered if . . ." She twisted her small body. "If you . . ."

"What?"

"I wondered if you might teach me."

Aha!

"I saw you make the fire. You knew I was up there all the time, didn't you?"

I nodded gravely.

"I'm a Mouse Spy, the best there is. But when I leave the Guard I want to be a mage, like you. Teach me! I will serve you well."

"Aefa," I said solemnly, "I have spirit servants. What service can you offer that they cannot?"

"Um." She twisted her small body thoughtfully. Then, "Spirits can't handle things. Real things. I can run and steal things for you. I can kill the white doe for you, that one over there."

"Don't do that. She and I are friends for now."

"Then I won't."

"What I want now, Aefa, is a gown for the Flowering Moon dance. Can you steal me a white gown?"

"Easily!"

"And an apple blossom crown."

"Right away!"

"The day after the dance I will show you the first step."

"What's the first step?"

"To be quiet."

"Oh." Disappointed. "Just to be quiet?"

"You will find that enough to learn. And, Aefa, I would like food tomorrow. Human food. Bread and cheese and . . . a nip of ale."

"As good as done!" Aefa smiled a surprisingly charming smile, and vanished. She was in truth a Mouse Spy. I could have vanished no more cleanly myself.

I turned back to my fire. I had lost time talking with Aefa; the fire was already dying. But in the sputtering ashes I saw a giant knight ride toward me on a great charger. Speared on his lance he carried a great red flower; he dipped his lance to me and I accepted the flower.

In the last embers I saw Dana. She stood as in the mosaic, hand on flower, back toward me. In a turning flame she turned to face me, and she was Elana.

My little fire fizzled. Black smoke drifted up and over me like Elana's cloud.

My brother had gone away, never to return.

I said this over and over. Firmly I told my heart, He will not return. If I could accept this the pain would pass through and beyond me. But my heart cried, No! No! And beat back the pain. And so the pain circled me like a serpent.

My world stood empty. Lugh had shone over my life as moon shines over forest, and I had not even known it! I shut my eyes, rocked from side to side and clenched my fists. Doubled over, I felt a light hand on my shoulder.

My spirit leaned over me and whispered, *Breathe.*

I breathed deeply. The spring air was real and sweet, though Lugh had gone away.

My spirit said, *Be quiet.*

"Is that all?" I asked. "Only be quiet?"

You will find that enough to learn.

A long time later I opened my eyes and saw the white doe still stepping about under the beeches, almost as quiet as a ghost.

<hr/>

White-robed and flower-crowned by Aefa, I perched on the lowest branch of a vine-laddered oak near the river. I watched the Flowering Moon rise, and listened to distant drums.

In glades from here to the west edge of the forest the Fey were gathering to dance. Their drums were soft, like heartbeats, not much louder than the crackling fires the dancers circle. They were coming by coracle down many a stream. They were coming on foot along many a game trail. I thought the Lady must be poling away from Avalon now, arrayed in shimmering robes, Merlin's best gifts. I thought that somewhere Elana must be moving toward the nearest drum, and breathed a spell for her, that some man at the dance might help her forget my brother.

If Mellias were here he would dance tonight in swinging otter skins and antlers. His eyes would glint this way and that, searching for me. Mellias had long desired me, and tonight I thought I might desire him. Throughout my body I felt a warming and softening I had never known before.

But Mellias was out in the kingdom playing Lugh's deaf servant. He might be lying in straw, or scrubbing crocks. He might not even see the Flowering Moon through the roof and walls around him! If he saw or felt the Moon he might bed some serving girl, like Yseult's "maid." But she had better beware, poor fool! Out in the kingdom the Goddess' best gifts can curse.

I wanted to make my way toward the nearest drum, but a voice in my head told me, *Wait*.

So I waited for I knew not what, sitting so still in the oak a passing owl brushed my face with his wing. I might have taken that for a warning.

Far off, three drums spoke and answered each other. Close at hand, a nightingale trilled. Beyond that, a threatening voice bawled.

Was it Fey, Human or animal? Did it come or go?

It yawped rhythmically, savagely, always nearer. I drew my feet up on the branch and wished my gown were dun-colored. I must stand out in shadow like the white doe.

Something crashed, thumped and panted through underbrush. Something rushed past under my branch.

My white doe. I glimpsed wide eyes and laid-back ears, I smelled terror. Three breaths later she splashed into the river.

The oncoming voice belonged to a hunting hound in full cry. I had never heard it before, for Humans did not hunt our forest. But I recognized it from stories. The hound might be lost and searching his own meat. Or Human hunters might follow him. How would either dog or hunters have passed the Children's Guard?

Gods, the Guard had gone dancing! It was left for me to handle this invasion, armed only with the knife in my belt.

I scrambled down the oak, plucked up my gown in both hands and ran to the river.

There swam the white doe upstream, silver head and shoulders trailing a silver wake. I called to her, "Sister, I guard the trail!" Standing astride her trail I drew my knife and faced the great hound that came rushing.

Nose to earth, baying, he ran almost into my feet. I had the knife ready to plunge when he jerked back, trembled and growled.

Underbrush cracked behind him.

The hound stood tall as the doe, dark-coated, stinking. I exerted my aura and let it stab the air, burning like green fire. I felt it tingle and glow, and the hound saw it. Puzzled, he drew back and crouched. This technique had turned boar and wolf before; I was pleased to see it work on a dog, who lives with Humans and might be harder to turn. But would it work on the Human who now stepped out of shadow?

No; for he, a mere Human, could not see my aura.

He came alone, one panting, sweating hunter, smelling like his dog; a big man, a giant. Sweat gleamed in his dark curls and beard. Metal gleamed at his throat, on his hands. He strode toward us, then stopped and made a hand-sign I did not then recognize. "God's blood!" he panted, and backed off two steps.

I stood firmly across his path, grinning open-mouthed, gown and teeth and ready blade glistening in moonlight. I was set to take him with my knife; I had marked where to stick it, and crouched to leap, when I saw his resolve crumble.

He paled, his mouth fell open. Again he hand-signed, sketching a magic design in the air between us, and drew back another step.

I knew then what he thought. I laughed open-mouthed. I need not sacrifice my life to take his. The wise deceptions of the Fey, practiced for generations on his kind, had disarmed him without a blow.

I could play with him. Quietly I asked, "Stranger, do you seek the dance?"

"Dance?" He held one hand out-stretched, ready to sign again. (Now I realized he was signing against evil, calling his Gods to his aid.) A great, heavy ring shone on his meaty third finger.

"You hear the drums. Do you seek to dance with the Fey?"

He shuddered visibly. "Lady." He gulped. "You know well that I seek the white deer. I will gladly give up that chase."

Now, that was a brave admission! Thinking I was myself the white deer, transformed—or she was me—he confessed to the hunt.

His courage interested me. I studied him. The drums beat, my blood stirred and beat; the Flowering Moon sailed high.

I need not go to the dance. Mellias would not be there. And here the Goddess had delivered a strong, handsome, terrified man into my hands. Human, to be sure. But I would be far from the first Fey to couple with a Human.

Now I smiled close-mouthed, sheathing my teeth. I glided to him and gripped his large wrist in both hands. He leapt like a shot hare. Sweetly I smiled up at him. "Come," I cooed, "you are tired from the hunt. Come with me and rest." I led him back to the great oak. His dog followed us, growling and whining.

Among the reaching oak roots we sat down together. My man was pale; his teeth were chattering. If he were to do much for me he would need reassurance. I leaned against his side and murmured, "Now. Tell me about you."

"About me."

"Not your name, I need not know that." His shoulders relaxed half a finger. He thought if I knew his name I could magic him anytime, from any distance. He was beginning to hope he might live through this.

"Tell me . . ." I was getting the solid feel of him now. Overwhelming. "How did you come here?"

"You know I followed . . . you."

"Did no one warn you?"

"Yes. Yes, I was warned. No one would follow me."

"Yet you came."

"Lady," he said with forlorn pride, "I am a warrior."

And so he was, in truth! I could not see his aura in the evening shadow, but it poured over me like a waterfall, vibrant, powerful, tingling. This was a Human hero. Merlin sang tales of just such men as this.

I murmured, "I led you here because I want you." And I stretched up and kissed his bearded cheek.

His shoulders slipped a bit looser. Hope—and energy—grew in him.

"Tell me now, Man, where are you from? Your speech tells me you come from far away." So did his moving aura, his ring, and the wide metal collar that almost circled his neck.

Sure now of my immediate intentions, he found voice. He fed me a wonderful story that Merlin should have sung, of humble beginnings and violent adventures, of a mage and a lady who gave him a magic sword, with which he killed nine hundred enemy Saxons in a single battle, and so became chief of his people.

I suspected he was no more the chief than I was the white doe. But the tale was true in spirit, he was a true warrior, such as Humans and bards admire. And I was a hotly eager virgin, and the moon sailed high, and the drums beat. I wound my fingers among his coarse curls. "And what do you do now?"

"I fight Saxons. Holding the Saxons back from our lands is my life-work."

The only life-work I knew belonged to women, daughters of the Goddess. The thought that a man might claim a life-work was new to me.

51

"I thought you killed all the Saxons."

"Always, more come."

"You always win these battles?"

"I would not be here if I did not."

And he was here, strong and warm, huge and foolish. His smell was not good, but the rising smell of my own lust covered that. Like most Humans, he probably carried fleas and lice. I could deal with those later.

Very courteously he asked me, "Is this what you want? You are sure?" For, of course, if he displeased me I could turn him into a hedgehog.

Vinelike, I twined around him. His dog lay down to watch us, head on paws. Far off the drums beat. Nearer, the nightingale sang.

⚜

The Lady Nimway took occasional Human lovers. Afterward she would send them straight into the small, cruel hands of the Children's Guard. "Walk north along the stream," she might say. "That will bring you out of the forest." And the man, who half expected to be turned into a stoat, would kiss her hands and walk north till a poisoned dart found his throat.

No Human lover of hers ever returned to his hearth, or to the wife watching for him at the door. No true tale of our forest and its trails ever reached the kingdom. For when we Fey deal this way with Humans, the rule is Love and Death. First love, then death.

At first light I rose on my elbow and looked my man over. Hair and beard were black, skin faintly brown; embroidered red and black dragons adorned his fine wool tunic; his collar was a golden torque. His sleeping aura pulsed, a strong, rich orange. Gods, I thought, Maybe he really is a chief! Well, never mind that. What do I do with him?

He woke. At sight of me his grey eyes jerked wide. He had expected me to vanish with the moon.

I laughed, close-mouthed. "I am still here." He sat up and looked down at himself. "You are still here," I assured him. No roots grew from his feet, nor wings from his shoulders.

Whining, his hound crawled toward him.

I said, "I will take you out of the forest."

He never blinked. Maybe he did not know the rule I was breaking. He said, "Tell me something."

"What do you want to know?"

"Outside this forest, is it today, or a hundred years from now?"

I did blink.

"Harpers sing of men who pass a night in . . . such forests. When they return to earth, a hundred years have passed."

I had never heard that good story! "Would that matter?"

"Well. In a hundred years without me, the Saxons might have won."

He took himself seriously, this maybe-chief. "Perhaps you would prefer to stay here?"

"Give me the Saxons."

I laughed, glad of my decision. He deserved to live. "I will take you out; but first, you must eat."

To allay any suspicion, I ate with him. We shared Aefa's stolen bread and cheese; but he alone ate Grand Mushroom, enough to bewilder three giants. Dizzying, he said to me, "Ask me a boon, Lady. Ask what you wish."

"You must have enjoyed the night."

"Ask quickly . . . I cannot keep awake . . ."

"You have given me my boon already." (I knew not then that I spoke but the truth.)

He tore the red-gleaming ring off his finger and pushed it down onto mine. It rolled around on my small finger, around and up and down. To save it I dropped it into my pouch with Gwen's hair and Mellias' crystal.

The giant's aura winked and shrank. The dog saw this and whined.

"He will do very well," I told the dog. "If you could tell what you know, I would feed you Grand Mushroom, too." The man was now too mazed to hear me.

Once in the coracle—half-stumbling, half-dragged—he slumped against the rim. His eyes slid shut. I climbed in, took up the pole and pushed off. Downriver we rode, the hound swimming behind us.

In the same opening, thinning woods where Elana and I had dressed Gwen, I pulled the coracle ashore and heaved my hero to firm ground. He sprawled. His dog pattered up, shook himself and stretched out beside him. My Human was well guarded.

I hesitated. This was a man of real power. Suppose, when he woke, he remembered!

Unlikely. He might remember one or more details of the night, but it would all seem like a dream. I felt sure that what he might remember could do us no harm. So I left him.

Standing, poling upstream, I laughed aloud. There was one hero who would chase no more white deer! I laughed richly, savoring the joke, and the joy of the night just past; and that was good, for I was not to laugh again soon.

Flocks of ducks rose, clapping their wings, before the coracle. Air was loud with bird-cries, water loud with rushing, morning light beamed and sparkled. Among tall reeds my white doe drank, her little white kid at heel. "We did well, sister," I told her. "You brought me my first lover. I saved your life. Be well now, you and your children." So I blessed her, not knowing I had the true power to bless, and poled on by.

Near my clearing I paused to lift my tunic and trousers from the overhanging branch where Aefa had hung them. For this service I would teach her the warts-off song.

I poled on toward Apple Island, Avalon, my home. I had made a hard peace with my brother's loss and my friend's weakness. I had cast aside virginity and known deep pleasure. I felt strong, gifted, fit. I hummed a poling song.

The river narrowed and flowed faster. Ducks thundered up before an unmanned coracle bobbing downstream.

Two swans glided beside the boat. One on each side, they pecked at greenery that trailed over the rim. The coracle was mounded with greenery and flowers. Gods, it was a floating garden!

Curious, I poled to intercept the drifting coracle. The boats bumped midstream. With one hand I leaned on the pole, with the other I gripped the floating garden's rim.

Down there, under flowers, on flowers, Elana lay asleep.

She was dressed for the dance in a bleached linen gown. Buttercups crowned her sunny brown hair that trailed on the sunny brown water. Her aura, pale already in the daylight, was a narrow, diminishing quiver of grey. "Elana? Elana!" My friend must have consumed six times the Grand Mushroom I had fed my man. When she floated past East Edge and into the kingdom, Elana would be dead.

Lugh had left her behind. So she had left him behind, forever. She had gone farther from him than he had gone from her. And she had made sure he would not forget her. Even if Lugh never saw her floating garden, he would hear of it. Harpers would sing this tale for years to come.

I said, "Elana. Lugh will forget you. At first he will wonder and grieve, but then he will turn back to his new life and forget. Do you think a little of Lugh's grief worth your life?" (And all the seasons ahead, Flowering Moons, babies, friends, lovers, feasts and fasts!)

Elana sighed.

"Elana." My arms ached, holding both coracles still in the current. "Elana," I said, "I will forget you, too. I must forget you. But I will always remember what you have shown me. Never, never, will I love any being the way you have loved Lugh!" I reached to touch her hand; my exhausted arms let the coracle slip. I muttered, "Elana, next time be born Human. You would make a much better Human."

And in my head I heard Elana answer, *I was.*

"Elana?"

Then I knew. Some Child Guard once leaned over a Human bed and lifted a sleeping infant away, and ran to sell it in our forest for

55

a new shirt, or maybe a boar-tooth necklace. Or maybe the bereaved Fey mother herself came gliding out from the trees at midnight to snatch away the baby. Or maybe the Human mother, herself, bore her child secretly at a forest edge and left it there. Humans normally have warm, commanding hearts, but I have heard tales. Elana was a changeling.

The revelation stunned me.

I knew from Merlin's tales that Humans sometimes lay their dead in flower-cloaked coffins. Elana's boat was just such a coffin. I leaned on my pole and watched the coffin and its attendant swans ride downriver.

Very soberly, then, I poled on home to Apple Island. Much had come to pass in a few days. But that morning, poling strongly upriver, I did not even know all that had come to pass.

I would have been even more sober had I known that even as I tricked and trapped my human lover, the Goddess tricked and trapped me. Her power flowed into my body on the tide of his seed. Now at this moment She sat in my center, spinning her dark, holy thread like a deeply satisfied spider.

The Goddess and I were one.

A Merlin Song

A near-grown child of herder folk,
A maiden, paused beneath an oak.
Watching her father's sheep, she stood;
A lad stole out from the mysterious wood.
A brown boy he, and small and quick,
His every move a twinkling trick.
All summer did those children play,
The herder-maiden and the Fey.

Then winter came. He slipped away,
And left the maid his debt to pay.
In hovel dark she bore her child
And named him for his father wild:
Merlin the Hawk. Her folk were glad
To raise a strong and clever lad—
Until his talents showed. He told
Dream-messages. He could unfold
The future written in a palm.
He could sing ballad, charm or psalm.
Then said his folk, "There's danger here!
We've raised a witch, a spirit-seer!
Though doubtless he can bless the herds
And read our fate in flights of birds,
Strong curses he can also give.
The boy's half Fey. Why let him live?

Then did his mother grieve and pray
And hoard each gold or rainy day;
She held him close, and kissed his face,
Each hour with him a thankful grace . . .

3

GODDESS

When the Goddess within me announced Her dark power and presence, I pretended I did not understand. I ignored Her, and sought some other, more acceptable explanation for my bodily symptoms and my dreams. I was yet very young, not ready to sacrifice to the Goddess. So I guarded Her secret from myself until it became obvious to the world.

Then said the Lady, "You pay your life-debt early! Well, that is good. Birthing is easy when you are young." (Birthing, easy? If that birth was easy, I never wish to see a hard one!) Naturally, she thought I had made deliberate sacrifice to the Goddess. After all, I was intelligent and well-taught. I should never have been "caught" pregnant, like an ignorant Human girl.

But caught I was. In my excitement, at the height of my adventure, I had simply been careless. I never confessed that awful truth to a soul, nor the worse truth, that my child's Human father yet strode the green earth!

My child! My dark, tiny boy! His skin was so soft, his smell so sweet, I wanted to eat him. His grey eyes, innocent as a fawn's, were his father's. His even-lengthed fingers and toes were mine. I bore him in a low sapling-tent near the lake, half-hoping that he would prove deformed or feeble. If he missed so much as a fingernail, I could drown him. I never expected the world to thrill and shake and reform itself at his first cry! I never expected to carry him home to the villa as the Goddess' finest gift to me, and my finest gift to Her world.

Proud after pain, delighted after bewilderment, I brought him home and treasured him, and named him Bran. Delighted, the Lady received him.

We laughed with him at the villa fire when every gesture, every gurgle fed laughter. We conversed brilliantly with him before he could talk. One bright morning, crawling across the Dana mosaic, Bran rose up and stood on soft feet.

The Lady gasped and crowed. My heart rose and bloomed, a tall flower. And again we laughed.

Bran learned to walk on the tiled villa floors where I had learned. He named his colors from the Dana mosaic where I had named them. Once walking, he followed me everywhere, reeling, falling, rolling down hillocks, scrambling among rocks. "M-Ma," he yelled constantly, like a lost lamb.

He trapped me. I despaired of invisibility or speed. With Bran at heel I walked for all the world like a Human woman, obvious as a tree, turtle-slow. Angrily I counted the moons that must pass before he could go free in the forest, and leave me free.

But then his cry of "M-Ma!" would tear at my heart and I would go back and pick him up, kiss him, smell his sweetness, devour him with love. So have I seen a bear cuff her cub head over heels, then embrace and nurse and kiss him.

Bran became a fine child, brown and leggy and bright, like a red deer calf. He was never ill. (Because we Fey live alone or in very small groups, illness is rare with us. Merlin taught me later that sickness is not a God's curse, as Humans believe. It is in truth a living being, an unseen child of the Goddess, who hunts his meat as we hunt ours. But we are his meat.)

Bran ran and learned faster than most Fey children. Earlier than most, he struck out on his own. No more did he struggle after me, calling "M-Ma!" like a lost lamb. He left me free to hunt eggs, braid reeds or invite visions. Little Bran pranced off by himself, eager, competent, nearly invisible as I had taught him to be, under the apple trees of Avalon.

In the evening he would skip across the Dana mosaic into our courtyard, swinging a duck by the neck or a rabbit by the ears. Still he crept under my cloak, stolen long ago off an aged Human's feet, to sleep with me on a cold night.

But I knew of the shelters Bran had built for himself around the island. Otter Mellias had shown me. (Since he never had Lugh's passion for the Human world, but only a yen for occasional adventure, the Otter spent as much time in Avalon as he did playing "Squire." He watched my son grow.)

"He builds well," Mellias declared, proud as though the child were his own. "Back to the wind, feet dry. Look, can you see that hut in the willows?" I shook my head. Mellias had to lead me to it and place my hand on it. It looked exactly like the surrounding thicket.

I should have rejoiced. In truth, I smiled proudly at Mellias, as though the child *were* his, but my heart sank. In truth, I felt abandoned. Bran did not really need me or my cloak at night. He came home now only from habit.

That night he was late coming home, and I watched the door anxiously.

The Lady said, "Let the child go, Niviene!"

"He is so small!"

"He is not a baby." She peered at me sharply. "Have yourself another baby."

Watching the door, I shook my head.

"If you do not want to sacrifice again so soon, steal one."

That brought my eyes back to her. "Steal?"

"Certainly. Human children often turn out quite well."

Several nights after that Bran did not come home at all. I could not sleep. Heavy autumn rain dripped through a new hole in the roof. I pictured my little one rain-swamped, maybe sitting in an apple tree soaked through, rain and tears mixed on his small face, waiting for daylight so he could slosh home.

Then I pictured him curled up squirrel-fashion in the tiny willow shelter Mellias had shown me or in one of several I had found myself. One leaned against a beech like a fallen branch. One humped in the lee of a big rock. Bran was most likely as safe and warm as I was myself, I thought, and I had better sleep, then go seek him in the morning. How far could a small boy go, after all? He was somewhere on the island. I turned over and felt his empty, cold space under our cloak, and wept.

At first damp light I visited Bran's shelters. Slipping and stumbling toward home I met Mellias returning from a good night's fishing. *Bran is gone,* I signaled him.

"Well." Bent under his net Mellias paused beside me. "That was a rough first night away! But that is how boys like it, you know. Niviene," he added kindly, "you are distressed. You have wept."

"Tell, and I'll turn you into a toad!"

Mellias laughed. He dumped his net, took my hand and turned with me toward the villa. He smelled of fish and mud and rain. I leaned against him.

"Don't take it so hard. Boys go free younger than girls."

"Not this young!" Bran was barely five.

"Well, you have a bright one. My first night out it was snowing. Wolf tracks all around me in the morning." Mellias led me along gently, steadying me with an arm around my waist.

A wet greenness ahead was the villa back wall. He let me go. "I'll wager you'll find your nestling drying his feathers at the fire. Be calm with him, Niviene."

"Well, naturally!"

"If he's not there, talk to your mother. She raised two of you. She knows."

I looked away. "I fear her scorn."

Mellias said, "Perhaps you misunderstand the Lady." Then he left me.

My nestling was not by the fire. I found the Lady in our room, searching through his pile of clothes. Many of these she had made herself, taught by a Human woman whose sick child she had healed.

She looked up almost guiltily as I entered. "I wondered if he took his cloak. He took so little, I think he will come back today. Enjoy your freedom. Remember how you longed for it?"

"Yes." Well did I remember the foolish girl-mother who ground her teeth at the hounding cry of "M-Ma!" I tried to enjoy my freedom that day and the next and the next.

On the fourth morning, a glad golden autumn morning, I crouched by the courtyard fire-stones, warmed my palms, and lit a small scrying fire. Kneeling over it I intoned, *Bran! Bran! Bran!* Snapping, the fire spoke of sun and rain, wind, snow, cool earth. "Bran!" I cried; and dropped tears into the fire.

Now the fire spoke briskly of several things. I saw three children in invisible cloaks swing through yew trees. I saw a boar splash into the lake and swim toward Avalon. I saw a winter-wise serpent slither into his hole under a rock.

The fire faltered.

Feet came softly about me. I looked up at the Lady, Mellias and Aefa. Aefa said, "The ravens told me to come."

I snatched at hope. What one could not see, maybe another could. I cried, "Aefa! Scry for Bran!"

She sank on her heels beside me. "You know, Niviene, he is at that age when children disappear."

"Not this suddenly! Not for four days at a time! Scry for Bran!"

The Lady stood over us, absently combing her hair with her fingers. Her eyes were red from crystal-gazing. "With all our scrying we should have seen him by now," she murmured. "Niviene, calm yourself. Excitement wastes power."

The little fire died.

Aefa sat back. "I saw him in the flesh, Niviene, not two days ago."

"Gods! Where? Why did you not tell me?"

"I did not know you sought him. He was passing under my tree-house, oh so skillfully, almost invisible. I thought, 'There goes a future Mouse Spy!'"

I stared at Aefa. Her tree-house was across the water. Had my little one swum the lake, like the boar scried in the fire? He was too small to pole a coracle.

She said, "He was headed north when I saw him. Then later, I heard talk about the north edge."

I leaped to my feet. "What talk?"

"Some sort of . . . power . . . had moved into that part of the forest and cast a shield around itself."

The Lady and I exchanged appalled glances.

"Birds and animals were seen to avoid the shield. Common Fey with no magic felt it and stayed away. It was there a day and night; then it lifted."

"But . . . Bran would stay away too!"

The Lady murmured, "Not if the power called him."

Mellias shifted uneasily. He was ready to beat the forest bush by bush, but this talk of powers and shields disturbed him. Mellias was young, then, as Aefa and I were young.

The Lady had not left Avalon for a season, except to visit the Human woman who taught her skills. Now she put on shirt and trousers, braided her hair and came with us. In two coracles we crossed the lake and poled up the north channel.

Mellias, poling ahead, cried out softly and dropped his pole.

Beside him, Aefa said, "Here's the shield."

We all felt it. My hair tried to rise and I shivered. A power struck through my body as lightning once struck Counsel Oak.

The shield was disintegrating, lifting away like shreds of fog. Poling hard we pushed through and left it behind. Behind us we left ducks and swans feeding; before us, no bird swam or dabbled. No fish rose to the surface. Yet in the shield-misted silence, something moved.

Mellias whistled like a blackbird and indicated with his head.

Among tall brown reeds moved something small and white. A white fallow kid poked his head from the reeds as though to greet us. Behind him a second white kid splashed in the shallows.

I jammed my pole into mud, stopping the coracle. I said, "I'll follow those twins."

The Lady nodded. "Take Aefa. Mellias and I will go on by water, search the banks."

Aefa and I splashed ashore and pulled my coracle in among the reeds. The kids scrambled up the bank and seemed to wait for us. They circled each other, looking at us over their shoulders and switching their tails. As soon as we joined them on the bank they moved away, still looking back; and we followed, almost within touching distance.

The northern edge of the forest had not been much lived in of late. We passed hidden abandoned huts and tree houses, and one dancing ring where young trees were beginning to take root.

The kids trotted and skipped before us. In the dancing ring they paused to play, bounding about aimlessly, as though forgetting their mission. Aefa called softly, "Pretty children! Guide us now, please." And they froze between one bound and the next, looking at us astonished. We walked slowly toward them; and when they were almost within our reach they leaped and trotted away single file, slowly enough for us to follow.

The north channel swings in a great arc around that edge of forest. The Lady told us later that it is not easy poling, what with shallows and falls and rocks. The twins led us more or less straight overland to rejoin the channel at the tip of its arc; there, in the first mud of the first swamp by the channel, they paused. Small heads high, ears a-twitch, they watched us come, skipping back just before we reached them.

There in the mud a clear footprint had sunk deep and almost solid. A clear, small footprint.

I sank to my knees beside it. I said, "His boots are wearing very thin." I stared into the footprint as though I could scry it, while Aefa cast about like a hound for more.

"No more," she said at last. "You'd think he had stepped once in the mud, then been snatched up by an eagle." But Bran was not quite that small. She added, "It may not even be Bran."

I shook my head. "I was looking for new boots for him. I knew they were thin."

I stood up, took a great breath and screeched, breaking the forest law for the first time since I was Bran's age. Aefa looked shocked. The kids leaped high and disappeared in a thicket, not to be seen again. "Bran!" I yelled, waking echoes from the old swamp trees. "Bran, come to me! Bran, come here!"

Somewhere in the dim swamp a disturbed owl hooted.

Aefa and I camped near the northern edge for several days. We scried and searched and found nothing, not so much as a thread from Bran's tunic.

Worn-out and heartsick, I went home to the villa. The Lady said, "I do not feel our Bran is dead, Niviene."

I looked at her wearily.

She continued, "To make sure, we two will call the dead."

I went cold. "Call the dead? We do that?"

"Indeed we do, when there is need. I will show you."

That night—a cold, windy night—we sat cross-legged in the courtyard holding hands. A small lamp burned between us. The Lady taught me a chant that we chanted softly, endlessly, while leaves and twigs blew out of the dark around us. "Chant," the Lady had told me, "until a ghost comes by. Look and see if it is the ghost you want. If not, do not move, do not speak to it, give it no power. Once you move or speak, the spell is broken."

We chanted till the maiden moon rose over the wall and the lamp burned low and we froze stiff where we sat. I had forgotten what we were doing; I think I thought I was dreaming when a new, sharper cold pierced my frozen bones and a dim, white shape drifted near.

I looked up at it almost incuriously, noting that it was not Bran.

It was a hefty, Human-sized maiden in a Roman-style gown. I thought, Dana! This was the spirit I myself had created in the villa in my childhood, my imaginary friend. I had not thought a secondary spirit, created by my thought, would endure so long.

Dana turned toward me then and I noticed flowers caught in her hair, which was drenched, and she seemed to drip water; and I thought again. Elana!

I stopped chanting and took a breath to speak.

The Lady gripped my numb hands so hard they hurt, and I quieted. Once you speak, the spell is broken. So Elana drifted past, shifting and changing and disappearing as she went, and we chanted on for a while.

My throat hurt. I could hardly mumble the chant, when from behind me floated the burdened old woman-ghost I had met in the villa before. She had not changed. Her thin face was still crumpled, her white hair bound back with a rag. On her bent shoulders she carried a load of . . . wash? I longed to speak to her, to say, "Poor ghost, you do not have to wash clothes here any more. Your life here was finished long ago. Be off, find yourself a new life, a better one! You are free to go." I bit my tongue so as not to speak.

Then came the child.

At sight of the small, flying form I would have started up; but the Lady held my hands. He flew slowly past, smiling, waving his plump, small arms like wings. His curls bounced on his shoulders. He rolled around once in the air, flying upside down.

He was not Bran. I had seen this ghost before, too, in my childhood. He was not Bran.

He fluttered by and the lamp burned out.

The Lady mumbled, "Our night is over." The maiden moon stood high in the sky.

Grabbing each other, leaning on each other, we staggered into the Lady's warm, smoky room, where a brazier burned. We stretched out together under her deerskins, and slowly we came back to life. Warmth crept back into our blood, intelligence into our eyes. We looked at each other. The Lady's face—still beautiful, very little lined—was wet with tears. She said, "You know, children can be lost at this age. It happens almost every year."

"I know." But till now, the lost ones had not been mine.

"You are young," my mother said. "You can have another."

"No."

"No?"

"I will never sacrifice to the Goddess again."

"Niviene!" Shock stiffened the Lady's face. "Quickly, take that back! Before She hears."

"It's too late." The Goddess had heard. I felt Her presence in the room with us.

The Goddess is always with us and in us. She breathes through us, sees through our eyes, hears with our ears . . . feels with our hearts. But we are only aware of Her with effort. When we feel Her presence like this, unasked, She means to speak to us. I listened.

Little One, I almost heard Her say, *You did not refuse the joys I sent you. Why do you refuse grief?*

I said aloud, "Because I would die of it."

Yes, She assented, *you will surely die. Love life while I live you, Little One; love summer and winter, joy and grief.*

Her presence faded like a sweet scent. I said quietly to the Lady, "From tonight I sacrifice no more. I live for myself alone. In the morning I will take my heart down to the lake and drown it, like a deformed child."

And so, in truth, I did.

Naked under my "invisible" cloak I came down to the lake shore, bare feet squishing cold mud, rain like tears on my face. I picked fallen leaves and twigs and vines, and from these I fashioned a coracle the size of my hand, and I breathed my living heart into this boat. Then I shrugged off my cloak and waded into the lake, freezing feet sunk in frozen mud. I waded till the near-icy water reached my thighs and stood there, breathing my power.

Slowly, power warmed my face, neck, shoulders and breasts. More slowly it warmed my hips and legs, and mud-sunk feet. At last I no longer felt the freezing water, but only the blazing glow of power.

Then I raised the little coracle, breathed into it once more and said, "Take my heart, with all its sorrow. Carry it away. Drown it." The leaf boat quivered in my cupped hands, and a dim grey aura rose around it, as of a living being. I set the little boat on the water and pushed it away.

I stood glowing in the lake as long as I could see the coracle ride the current. Quickly it disappeared among small, choppy waves; but I could see its grey aura twirling along. I stood there till it was completely gone, disappeared and swallowed up.

Then power faded and intense cold rushed into my body. I scrambled out of the lake, seized my cloak and rubbed myself warm before slinging it on. Only then did I pause to listen to my heart.

I heard nothing, not a gurgle, whimper or sigh, because I had no heart. I had a softly beating drum in my chest that marked the moments of my life; but the heart that felt and remembered, grieved and rejoiced, was gone. I had drowned it.

Turning home, I hummed a morning song.

After that my life was easy. Following Merlin's counsel I lay alone and reaped great power. Heartless, one does not suffer.

But neither does one enjoy. Life can become almost a burden. But Merlin cured that.

4

FLIGHT

Merlin said kindly, "Child. Out in the kingdom, Arthur's Peace is endangered. I need an assistant mage to help me assure the common good, and you are among the best I know. Come out there with me."

The busy distaff paused in the Lady's hand. (She was learning the clothing arts from a Human witch whose sick child she had saved.) We huddled together in her villa room where snow did not leak in. By low lamplight we stared up at Merlin like owl nestlings, discovered.

I said, "Merlin, I would not care if your Arthur were crucified like his God." (Merlin had sung us that story.) "Why, in the name of all Gods, would I leave my hearth in winter and travel into the Human kingdom for Arthur?"

Merlin wriggled his brows. He said, "You will care if his Peace is broken. The Saxons will turn your forest into a sheep pasture."

The Lady murmured anxiously. She had long feared this very

thing, and so had I. What if the Angles out there learned that our forest was guarded, not by enchantment, but by children with poisoned darts? And they would learn, if the Saxons drove them into our arms.

I gazed into the lamp-flame and saw vast distances, alarming bare vistas under snow clouds. I asked, "How would I go out there and return? For I would not be crucified myself."

"Hah!" Merlin cried, victorious. "That I will show you!"

That very twilight, Merlin and I stood in falling snow at East Edge and held out our hands to a herd of winter-coated ponies.

They watched us cautiously. A brown mare shook her rough mane and pushed between us and her foal. The stallion pawed snow and snorted.

I thought of Mellias and his first dance with horses. I had no wish so to entertain the Guard children who must be watching. Mellias had danced with subdued slave-horses. These ponies were wary and free, not a halter among them, and no way to get or stay astride.

I signaled Merlin, *That stallion is angry.*

Not angry. Anxious. We will calm him. And Merlin began to sing.

At first he hummed under his breath. The ponies twitched their ears toward him. He sang softly, then clearly, then confidently. He signaled me, *Sing.*

I sang insincerely. I had no real wish to attract these heavy-hoofed creatures. Longingly I thought of the dry, warm room back in Lady Villa, with lamp and blankets and stolen bread laid by. The comforts of sorrow. My voice quavered; I drew back even as I sang.

Merlin signaled, *Stand here by me. Think of one horse—the brown mare. She is like you. Imagine she comes to you, like drawn to like.*

The ponies stretched ears and noses toward us. Snow built up on their coats as they faced us, and on our heads and shoulders as we sang. We must have looked like the snow creatures children make in hard winters.

Slow step by cautious step, the ponies moved toward us.

When they began to move it was dusk, and they were brown and grey, speckled and black. When they came snuffling around us, stamping and whisking their tails in our faces, it was night and they were all black.

They smelled greasy and warm. One pushed against me and breathed warmth down my back. Merlin whispered, "Catch her mane." And I, hardly believing, reached and laid hold of her bristly, mangled mane. Merlin whispered, "Mount." I hugged her strong neck and scrambled onto her back—assisted with a shove from Merlin.

Merlin whispered, "Sing!"

Singing, I settled down on the mare's back. Her strong, earthy aura, invisible in the darkness, tingled through me. Suddenly I was warm and large; coarse food gurgled in my belly. My thick coat held off snow and cold. I hardly felt the small weight on my back. I farted, shook my mane, smelled my foal and my companions around me. The wind from behind us brought smells of pig, dog, man, smoke, shit. These safe, known smells came from behind; before me, the windless darkness told me nothing. I turned and moved into the wind.

I, Niviene, clung to the mare's mane and swayed to her motion. Another mare moved close beside us. Perched on her back, Merlin said to me, "Sing, Niviene, and wrap the mare's spirit in your Fey peace."

Hah, that was the trick! I had let the mare's spirit wrap mine. Now I enlarged my own aura and threw it over and around her like a huge cloak. Her innocent mind yielded at once.

Singing, we rode through the night. I learned to turn the mare, to stop or start her with a touch and a thought. Singing, we left the herd and crossed dark fields, now into the wind, now cross-wind, the five of us our own herd: Merlin and his pony, I and my pony, and the foal trotting around us. The dim winter first light found us a long way from any place I knew of. In a valley meadow between wooded hills, Merlin said, "Hush now." And we stopped singing.

My throat, hips and legs ached ferociously. To my surprise the ponies did not throw us off. They were used to us now. Released from enchantment, they pawed the snow in search of grass. The foal pressed to my mare, trying to nurse. When she found a patch of grass and stood still, he succeeded.

Fearful now, I looked around this vast open space in which we were plainly visible. "Merlin," I croaked, "where are we?"

Merlin mumbled and twisted. "Don't know," he admitted. "Lost track. But the ponies will take us back."

In the new light I saw his mare's aura, a deep brown glow close around her; and I saw that she missed the herd, and would gladly return to the Fey forest's edge.

"Merlin, we'll be seen. There's not so much as a bush to hide behind!"

"Do like this." Merlin flopped down flat on his pony's neck. From any distance he would be invisible. Aching in every muscle, I lay down flat.

"Now," he said, spitting out horse-hair, "think of the herd."

I thought of the small herd we had left behind. I thought of the stallion, who must want us by now.

My mare stepped away from the nursing foal. She blew, swished her tail and started walking. Lying low, we rode back as the light strengthened. We passed thin woods, snowy meadows and several villages, where Humans stirred fires and trudged through the snow with milk pails. All these things we saw from a strange height, as though we were Guard children, perched in walking sentinel trees.

Outside the last village we paused at a hayrack set out for cattle. An angry man pointed us out to a band of idle boys who rushed screeching toward us, waving sticks. My mare started, shied and plunged into a headlong gallop.

Now did I learn to ride.

Flat-pressed to her straining neck I held on like a ferret. Earth and snow flew past beneath us. *Thunk-thunk*, we rushed toward East Edge. I heard the foal's small hooves drumming behind us, and farther back the thudding gallop of Merlin's mare. Wind sang around us, sun broke through snow-clouds. Had I breath I would have laughed for joy.

Danger left behind, my mare slowed to a canter, and a trot, and a walk. At last she stopped and looked around for the foal. He trotted up, fluffy tail whisking, one thought milky in his mind. Merlin came right behind him.

"Merlin!" I gasped. "There is the forest!" It loomed ahead, a darkness of close, bare trees and thickets. Home! In my relief I sat up stiffly, careless of pain and of who might see me.

Merlin caught his breath and said, "Now you know why Humans use bridles. And saddles."

"In truth! I have never moved that fast in my life."

"But you will move faster next time."

"I will?"

"You have forgotten why you are here."

"I must have. Quick, let us get into the trees." While the foal nursed, I slid down from the mare and collapsed.

Merlin dismounted and pulled me to my feet. "Can you stand, Niviene?"

"I . . . no."

He heaved me up in his arms and plodded toward the trees. I lay in his arms like a baby, looking over his shoulder.

Puzzled, the three ponies watched us leave. They stood together, furry-brown against white fields. As we left them behind a cord broke between us, and I lost touch with my mare. She became again an animal, alien, closed into her world as I was closed into mine. For now, we had nothing more to say to each other. She swished her tail and turned her back.

Merlin staggered in among the trees and let me down.

He made us a camp just within East Edge. We could look out through pine boughs at the kingdom. For a day and a night I could barely move, and Merlin cared for me as if he were a Human father.

I sent out a silent call to Aefa, and she found us at noon. She had the right herbs ready in her pouch. "What in the name of all Gods were you doing?" she asked in wonderment, massaging my hips.

"Riding. All night. Ah, that's better!"

"Riding?"

"Ponies."

"Ponies!" Aefa squeaked.

Outside the shelter, Merlin laughed. "You can join us next time, Aefa. You and Mellias."

"I? I am young yet, Merlin. I still have the use of my wits."

"Niviene and I are going out into the kingdom. To do that you have to ride."

"Hah!" Till that moment I had forgotten the reason for last night's adventure.

Like a bear testing a new den, Merlin pushed his head and shoulders into the shelter. "It will be good for you, Niviene. Consider. What thought never crossed your mind last night?"

"Last night. Keep doing that, Aefa! Last night I thought of nothing but horses."

And then I saw it. All night I had not once thought of my dead heart. Merlin raised a brow and nodded. "You see. The kingdom is the place for you now. And for you, Aefa. Mellias would delight in your company."

We rode together many nights that winter. Mellias was at home, and he gladly taught Aefa to ride using bits and reins, for he could not guide a horse with magic. Sometimes we rode two and two, sometimes four together like a charging army. On those nights hoof-beats rang over the frozen country, and Human folk turned on their pallets and muttered, "The Good Folk ride tonight."

At first we rode the half-wild ponies we could sing to. Later, we took to borrowing well-trained, well-combed horses from farm stalls.

One night I crept into a stable at dusk to find a farmer and his small son busily hanging rowan branches and stick crosses from the beams and from the grey gelding's halter. I melted into the wall. The boy asked, "Why would the Good Folk steal our Dobbin?"

"They been stealing horses out of barns. Horses limp home come morning with elf-locks in their manes, all wore out. But they won't get our Dobbin."

"Why not?"

" 'Cause of these here rowan and crosses."

"Why?"

" 'Cause the Good Folk are scared out of their skins at rowan and crosses. Ask me another 'Why' and I'll show you."

(The next morning, Dobbin ambled home all worn out, his mane a nest of elf-locks. After all, I had to hold onto something.)

5

KINGDOM

Counsel Oak towers over all the apple trees of Avalon; and from his topmost branches you see all of Avalon, and the bright island-circling water, and the dark-forested, lake-encircling shores. You see our world.

But as I once reminded Elana, there is another world beyond ours, encircling ours; and it circles outward forever.

At first it is villages, manor farms, woods framing fields, with here and there a finger of heavy forest. (And a very few of these forests are guarded, like ours, by brown children agile as squirrels, shooting poisoned darts from treetops.) But always you find an open track through woods and between forests, leading to other fields, manors, villages; with here and there a chief's dun, guarded by earthworks; and here and there a cross-crowned monastery, thatched huts circling a thatched chapel.

In the chapels stand Christian Gods and Goddesses and their winged servants, ready to step from their pedestals and waylay you—except that they are carved from wood. Like the Dana mosaic back in Lady Villa, they are the astonishing works of Human hands.

In the fields dig leather-tough men and women. In my childhood I knew such folk; I watched them from the shadows of East Edge; I robbed them by night, slipping easily through their yards, barns and huts. One night I danced with them, my hands clasped in theirs, breathing in their breath and odor.

Now I know who they are. Like rocks, bones of the Goddess, they uphold their world. These are the folk who fell great trees to build chiefs' halls, who raise earthworks around duns, who plant and harvest grain for Humans and Fey. These are the folk who beat out swords in fire, who herd and train knights' chargers and farmers' donkeys. The Human world rides on their stooped shoulders. (And we Fey ride, feather-light, atop the Human world.) For fifteen years I have traveled through the Human kingdom, ahorse and afoot, usually disguised as a twelve-year-old boy (always with Mellias' crystal dangling inside my shirt). I have lived at times in the King's dun, behind and under his earthworks, disguised (less successfully) as a Human lady. But out there in the kingdom my spirit is still a deer, a white doe, frightened and far from cover. I pause continually, mid-stride, to glance in all directions. My nostrils distend, seeking distant smells; my ears practically twitch. In truth, the Human capacity for hate and anger, for reasoned and unreasoned violence, still appalls me.

Humans imagine us Fey as dangerous. Compared to them, we are simple wild creatures that bite when cornered. Humans love a few of their kind—usually one or two—with extraordinary passion. Their hate is equally passionate. I have seen the ashes of Angle villages burned by Saxons, simply because they were not Saxon. I have seen the ashes of one Angle village burned by Arthur's own knights, who for some reason fancied themselves insulted. Riding with Merlin, my heart used to leap into my throat when armed horsemen drew near us on the trail. They were probably indifferent, sometimes friendly. But you could never tell till they had passed.

At the end of our first day's ride, Merlin drew rein before our first tavern. Aefa and I sat our tired ponies, equally tired ourselves, hunched down fearfully in our boys' clothes and "invisible" cloaks. (But out here invisibility was impossible. This fact frightened us more than the actual giants we had passed on the road.)

Merlin dismounted and stood looking at the tavern. I saw him feeling himself in our boots, wondering how fearful we would find it. He sighed, squared his shoulders and signaled to us to tie the ponies to the rail provided. Then he marched boldly to the door.

All day we had not been so far away from Merlin! We exchanged a glance, and Aefa's fingers asked me, *Shall we go in there?* My fingers said, *What else can we do?* We trailed Merlin like a pair of exhausted hounds.

Having lived at Lady Villa I was used to walls, floors, ceilings. Aefa told me later that following Merlin through that door was the hardest thing she had ever done. She felt like a fox creeping into a trap.

We were used to smoke and cooking smells—but not as thick as here! Never, sneaking into the filthiest village hut, had breathing turned me so dizzy!

But the giants—the monsters seated at tables or hurling darts, each shouting to be heard over the other, one stinking of manure and another from tanning, and all from ale, and none bathed in a season—the giants froze me with fear. I had stolen among many such who lay unconscious in the dark; but to walk visibly among them, to actually push past them, brushing their stiff sleeves in Merlin's wake, needed all my resolve.

At one point I stiffened, trembled and stopped. Aefa (terrified of walls and roof) set a small hard fist in my back and pushed. Merlin led us to sit at a shadowed corner table out of the way. Then he made to leave us. Aefa gasped, "Merlin!"

He paused, looked down and saw how it was with us. *I'm going over there*, he signaled. *Food. Ale. You sit quietly.* He left us.

We sat at that table like two brown doe hares in brown bracket, circled by hounds. We twitched no whisker. Between us and Merlin the giants roared and hurled their darts. They were good at darts. That was the first thing I noticed as breath came slowly back to me. They might win a game or two off the Guard children, or even off Aefa and me!

They paid no attention to us. Gradually I realized we might as well be wearing "invisible" cloaks; two half-grown children offered no entertainment or diversion to the giants. They had their own children, gratefully left at home.

Merlin came back with two chickens, three small loaves and ale. Fear-stiff as we were, we yet fell upon the food. And as we ate and drank and our warming bodies warmed our wet clothes, I began to watch the giants and listen to their uproar.

They shouted a coarse Angle with an accent I had not overheard before. But I am quick with languages. As I chewed and listened, I made slow sense of it.

They were arguing about the spring planting and the endless rain. One could not plant till the rain stopped. Would it ever stop, or had God decided to drown the world again? (Again?) Another feared that seed already planted would rot. A third rumbled, "It's the Goddess doing it!"

"Aye!" several voices growled agreement. "Because of the Queen. The Queen and her . . ."

"The fancy man!"

"That best knight the rest of them don't dare breathe on."

"And the King. What's he stand by and watch it for?"

"It's rotting him like rain rots seed."

"It's rotting his kingdom."

"And what becomes of us, then? When the high folk anger the Goddess?"

"The Saxons, Man. That's what becomes of us. You remember, when your home is a pile of ash and your family under it—remember to curse the Queen."

A twanging ripple of music sliced the noise.

Aefa and I exchanged alarmed glances. Without our noticing,

Merlin had left us alone among the giants and taken a stool by the fire, where he now tuned Enchanter on his knee; those jangling untuned notes silenced the giants.

One murmured, "I seen that harper before."

Another answered, "That be the mage harper. Whisht, now."

When Arthur first took the crown
Mage Merlin led him to a magic lake.
And from this lake rose an arm,
Call all in shining white samite;
And in its hand offered a sheathed sword.

Deep and mysterious sounded Enchanter, rippling like lake water.

And Merlin said, "Go. Accept yon sword."
Young Arthur hesitated—as who would not?—but
He was the son of Uther Pendragon.
Royal blood flowed in his veins.
He splashed into the lake and took the sword, and the
Arm clad in white sank back under the water.
Arthur drew the sword and waved it, all sunbright, and
Came back to Merlin on the shore.

Merlin said, "This is the magic sword,
Caliburn, who always draws blood.
And this is his sheath, even more precious,
For he who wears this enchanted sheath,
However wounded, will never bleed."

Then Arthur marveled. And Merlin said,
"The Lady of the Lake gives you Caliburn
To drive the Saxons from our land.
The day you fail your people, young king,
She will require him back from you."

This song hushed all talk of the King and his honor, for Caliburn still hung in his hall, as everyone knew; and the Saxons had not returned, praise God and blessed Mary. (Mary?)

Next, Merlin began a graceful ballad about the fair Elaine . . .

Who died for love of Sir Lancelot,
Arthur's best knight, and floated downstream
In a flowery barge . . .

The giants began to squirm and wave for more ale, and Merlin switched to a merry Miller's Daughter ballad. And while they bellowed the chorus and banged the tables, the harper vanished from his fireside stool.

Next morning, riding through rain and mud, I asked Merlin, "This Lancelot. Arthur's best knight. Is he real?"

"Is he real?" Laughter crinkled Merlin's eyes. "Is he real! Niviene, Lancelot is your brother Lugh!"

I almost fell off the pony.

"You did not know? You heard so many Lancelot stories, and you did not know?" Aefa nudged her pony up beside me and signaled, *What am I missing here?* Merlin spoke to her across me, "You remember one Lugh, son of the Lady, who went adventuring into the kingdom?"

"And never came back. Yes. He and Niviene were brother and sister and they knew it. I envied them."

"Niviene did not know that Lugh is now Sir Lancelot, Arthur's best knight."

"Ah." Tactfully, Aefa studied the mud her pony squelched through. "I did not know that either. So the crazy maiden in the song—Elaine the Fair. She died for love of *Lugh?*"

"You called her Elana."

True to my word to her, I had all but forgotten Elana. Even Elaine's flowering barge had not quite reminded me. Now again I saw the flowery coffin float downstream, swan-guarded. I saw myself poling home to Apple Island, grieving for my brother and my friend, so innocently unaware of the power waking and stretching within me!

~~❦~~

All this I now remembered clearly, riding between Merlin and Aefa through spring rain, on my first venture into the kingdom.

To help Merlin save Arthur's Peace, and our forest with it, I had learned to ride. I had learned Angle and Latin, Human custom and courtesy. I hoped to forget Bran out here in the kingdom, and for the most part I did forget. But sorrow waited for me in ambush. Sorrow might surround me at a word, or a harp chord plucked, or a familiar face.

Merlin brought us to Arthur's dun.

The dun was a huge, circular village. Small dens built of wicker, or wattle and daub lined planned, circular streets full of hurrying Humans. A massive earthen wall, a mountain, higher than the dens, higher than King's Hall in the center, encircled the whole. Like Lady Villa, this mountain had been built by Human hands. I accepted this as fact, astonished as my child-self had been by the villa's history.

By now we had passed through many villages. We trusted our disguises, and Merlin's guidance. Yet, to enter this great dun through the guarded gate, we called upon courage we did not know we had. Courage is a Human trait.

Merlin led us first to the stables, where we left our ponies in Human hands. On foot now, and trapped within the earthwork wall, we followed Merlin to his wicker hut that crouched beside the wall. Within, the hut reached down a tunnel some way back into the wall.

The hut was almost bare. Beside a central hearth several sleeping pallets were stacked. But around the walls stood chests, carved with pictures from Merlin's many stories. (I saw Tristam and Yseult pictured there, Queen Boadiccea, giants, dragons, Romans, Christian saints—and little figures meant to be Fey.)

Out of these chests Merlin brought bright, new gowns, such as those he gave to the Lady. Together, Aefa and I gasped and drew back.

"Come, dress yourselves," he invited us, holding out embroidered folds. "You must weary of being little boys."

I swallowed surprise, mingled with surprising desire. "But . . . all those Humans out there . . ."

"When we travel the world," Merlin told us, "you must be boys. But this is King Arthur's dun, civilized center of the kingdom. For you to disguise your sex here would insult Arthur and his Peace."

That same day, Merlin brought me to King's Hall, in the center of the dun. Dressed now daintily in a white gown, crowned with mistletoe, I paused in the great, carved doorway. The hall was the largest building I had yet seen, or have yet to see. No Fey could have simply entered it, unhesitating, as Merlin had strictly commanded me to do. I paused like a vixen before a trap, sweeping the immense space with cautious eyes.

At the famous round table in the midst of the room, Arthur's knights ripped bread and meat and tossed bones to waiting hounds. Merlin had designed this table round as the sun so that none who sat there could claim that he sat in a higher or more prestigious spot than another. All were equal. Fey would not have given that matter a thought; naturally, all the Goddess' children are equal. Fey would also not have gathered at that table, tens together, wolfing food and shouting so that the hall echoed.

On a dais above and behind the table, the King sat enthroned; on the wall above him hung sheathed Caliburn, the magic sword in his magic sheath; beside him, a round, bright-painted shield.

Merlin was pacing past the round table toward the King. He felt me not behind him, paused, and turned. His eyes flashed annoyance. He had bade me not hesitate, to walk directly behind him, head high, looking only at the King.

Hesitating still, I grasped the carved doorpost. The enclosed, airless place stank of Human sweat and roasted flesh. The hounds stank of blood. Great growling beasts, taller than the wolves they chased, they glared up at me from their bone scraps and rumbled deep in wide chests.

I raised and cast wide about me a silver cloud like a veil, like a cloak; and one by one the hounds silenced and shrank. I let loose of the doorpost. I lifted the hem of my gown up above the dirty strewn rushes and stepped slowly forward.

Arthur's knights gaped at me over the bones they gnawed. Those whose backs were toward me swung around to see, goblets in hand. They could not see my silver cloud. What they saw was a small, brown maiden robed in white, white berries caught in her flowing black hair. And they saw their hounds, who should be roaring around her, silent and still. And they saw Merlin, the King's honored mage, impatiently awaiting her; and like the dogs, they fell silent.

But as I glided past them through the new, heavy silence, lifting the hem of my gown, an odor I knew well arose from each and every giant body. Ordinarily I count the smell of lust no insult. But rising, as it did then, from tens of giants together, it startled me. Even frightened me. In truth, my heart stood in my mouth.

These were big men even by Human standards. Many of them carried famous names, known to bards. Their combined aura was an orange fire that filled the shadowy hall—except for the King's dais. That dais was haloed in triple lights.

Drawing near, I felt Mellias' crystal suddenly warm at my throat, and the pouch at my girdle suddenly heavy. One of the keepsakes within had stirred to life. I could not tell which one. But it dragged on me so that I slowed, and Merlin beckoned impatiently.

I glanced up then at King Arthur. He sat massively, ringed hands square on red-robed knees, watching me approach. Close around him his aura glowed red as his robe. A broad orange band circled the red, and a huge golden mist circled the orange, as wide as Merlin's white mist.

I looked within the triple aura at the King's strong face, into his hard, grey eyes. I stood rooted. Merlin, mounting the dais steps, turned and beckoned me, scowling.

I heard soft drums. A nightingale sang. Something long forgotten stirred in my body, delicious, tingling warmth. I thought, Holy Gods! A good thing it is in truth I did not poison you when I should have!

Slowly I paced forward and mounted the steps beside Merlin.

"This is my assistant," Merlin declared in elegant Latin, "Mage Niviene, come here with me to serve your Peace." So calmly did Merlin say this, and with no sidelong looks or nuances, that I knew he did not know Arthur and I had ever met before. Things did happen in the world, in the forest, that Merlin did not know. This was the first time I was sure of it.

A smile creased Arthur's eyes. He said, "You are welcome, Mage Niviene. Merlin has praised you to me before now. I think you are truly a great mage." Well did he know that! Had he not seen me as white doe and as maiden in the same night, with those same smiling eyes? He added, "I look forward to frequent . . . and enjoyable . . . consultations with you."

I tipped my head back and gave him a clear, level glance with a clear, definite message.

There I stood before his throne, surrounded by his giants and hounds, and I dared send him that look! He blinked. And power rose up in me, the power which I bought every day with my life, and I shone forth, and watched Arthur's triple aura tremble and draw back before mine.

(Merlin told me once, "If you wish to be a mage's mage, lie always alone." Merlin himself lay always alone. The Lady had taught him that, when she was ready. She herself did not make that sacrifice, and that was why Merlin, her student, eventually out-magicked her.

She did not teach me. Maybe she was waiting for me to bear a second child. But this I would never do. Never again would I sacrifice to the Goddess. She had given, She had taken. Let Her give and take no more.

I sacrificed now to my own power; Her power for mine. All the Goddess' energy that wanted to flow into the enjoyment and crea-

tion of life now flowed into power. I could sing the wild forest creatures to my hand. At my blessing an apple tree bore double fruit. I
could look now into Arthur's eyes and read his thoughts.)

Arthur was thinking, *The white doe flies from me again.*

I looked farther, into his heart.

At first I saw there a great and marvelous virtue, of which we Fey
are incapable. Arthur truly loved his people, all his people, his Gods
and his land. Gladly would he give his life for them.

Next, I saw that Arthur's soul was like the world, or the forest,
where life flourishes in the debris of death. He was entirely conscious of his exalted place in the Human world. His enormous third
aura expressed self-adoration, as well as virtue. Watching it burn
now against my own defending, expanding aura, I vowed to myself
that I would never challenge his self-adoration. I might not survive
such a challenge. Our positions were definitely reversed. Whereas
before we had met on my ground, where I held power, now the
power lay in Arthur's hands.

Meekly I said, "Lord, the magic we will perform for you must take
all our energy. For the sake of this magic we must renounce all dal-
liance and . . . pleasure."

Arthur relaxed, leaned back and smiled. "I shall remember that,"
he assured me. But he thought, *When she is ready, the white doe will
turn again.*

He raised a finger and a page-boy skipped to his side. "Lead Mage
Niviene to Queen's Hall," Arthur murmured. The page darted a look
at me and paled. I smiled to him, close-mouthed. I did not want
him frightened of me. A little fear can be useful; too much can block
one's path. I wanted the Humans I met to respect me, but not to the
point of silence.

"Merlin," Arthur said, "remain here. We have news of the Holy
Grail." He nodded a courteous dismissal to me, grey eyes smiling;
and the awestruck child led me away.

Out in the sun we chatted together as he guided me through
winding streets to Queen's Hall; by the time we arrived there the
skip was back in his step, and the ruddy color in his face.

⚜

King Mark, of whom Merlin sang, drew his sword.

Stitched in bright, soft threads on a huge dark canvas, Mark bent over Tristam and Yseult, asleep on the ground. A shaft of gold-threaded light picked out the King and the guilty pair, while all around them curled a cavern of dark threads, framed in golden light and blue-threaded vines.

Mark bent low, studying the sleeping faces. He saw Tristam's unsheathed sword asleep between the lovers, guarding them from each other. Silver threads defined the sword, and a silver aura around it.

His own sword in hand, Mark paused. You could see his dark eyes brood, wondering. A moment more, and he would back away, sheathe his sword, and leave the lovers in peace, for now.

I had wondered before now about this scene. Did the lovers truly keep the sword between them? Were they trying to conquer the powerful love-spell that doomed them? Or had they heard the hoof-beats of Mark's charger in the wood? Had they cast the sword between them and feigned sleep, rather than fight Tristam's Lord, whom he should have loved more than life?

I tore my fascinated gaze from the tapestry. I had seen pictures in Lady Villa. I was no longer amazed by Human art; though I had never seen any on this scale before, yet I was able to look away and examine Queen's Hall, open before me.

Several large tables and looms stood about, and baskets of wools and flax; and a crowd of richly dressed women, who gossiped across flashing distaffs. They silenced as we entered and looked at me eagerly. Their auras, discernible in the soft, indoor light, quivered like leashed hounds shown a scent. They thought I might be about to join them, to spin or card and tell them news of the larger world.

I glided past them on the young page's heels.

My pouch dragged heavily again. Another keepsake had stirred to life. The page led me to the far window where a woman sat spinning alone in a shaft of sunlight.

The Queen looked at me. The distaff stilled in her hand and dropped into her embroidered lap. I stood before her, smiling closed-mouthed; she stared at me, sensuous lips fallen a little apart.

Her body had firmed. Her long plait, draped over one sloping shoulder, still gleamed bronze. Green and orange, faint in the sunlight, her narrow aura clung to her form and nestled in the folds of her white tunic and embroidered overgown. Looking straight at me, she thought, *This small person. I have seen her before, maybe in a dream? This little dark one is dangerous.*

Spread-kneed she sat in the sun staring at me, her lap a flowered meadow between mountains, her distaff forgotten. The braided strands of her hair I yet carried in my pouch weighed me down so that standing straight was becoming difficult.

I said, "My Lady. I am Niviene of the Lake, Merlin's assistant. You know my brother, Sir Lugh—Lancelot."

Lugh's background was mysterious. No one here questioned him about it, and I hoped no one would question his sister. But at the name Lancelot, Gwenevere started. A red splotch glowed in her gold-freckled face. From her body arose a great cloud of scent, as though one had stepped into a garden of rose and honeysuckle. The women behind me gasped as one, then quickly fell to chattering like sparrows. Gwenevere raised a hand to her throat. Huskily she said, "You are welcome . . . Viviene . . . of the Lake."

"Niviene, my Lady."

"Are you staying with us long?"

"As long as I am needed."

I suspected I would not see much more of Gwenevere during my stay, and in that I was right. She feared and avoided me, though she could never remember where we had met before. But I learned what I needed to know from her there and then, in that brief meeting. I read every flicker of her pale lashes, every quick breath; I read her mind.

In her mind lived one entity, one concern: Lancelot. Not Lancelot/Lugh in himself, a being apart from her, but Lancelot/Gwenevere, a relationship. As for Arthur and his Peace, they meant no more to her than a fine sunny day, a pleasant background for more important matters.

I could not reach out to her in words. Her narrow, focused mind was impervious to words. I could not plant thoughts directly into her mind; they bounced off the surface of her constant concern with Lancelot/Gwenevere. She had something like an energy-shield around her mind. The energy trapped within could have made her powerful. But Gwenevere did not guess that. More than my child-hood friend Elana, Gwenevere was blind and deaf to the spirit.

I watched her, listened to her brief, meaningless talk, and thought, A pity she has no child. Sterility has twisted her heart thin, like her braid in my pouch. A pity she has no care for Arthur, or his people, but lives totally in her lovely body. A pitiful truth.

Later I returned to our hut under the great round earthen rampart that guarded Arthur's dun. The rampart had one obvious gated, guarded entrance-tunnel. There were also several hidden, unguarded tunnels, some incomplete. An hours' work with ax and pick could open one of these to the outer world. The hut assigned to us mages was built across such an incomplete tunnel. Its door faced the street and the dun; a back door opened into the tunnel. I swept in by the front door, gestured to Merlin and Aefa, and marched on out the back door, into the dark tunnel. Any word said in the hut could be heard in the street but no sound escaped from back here under the rampart. Here, we thought, was the place for magic, spells and sorcery.

Cunning Aefa brought a taper out with her, so I saw their eyes question me as we stood close together.

I said to Merlin, "It is as you say. The woman is mad."

Merlin nodded. He drew his knife and sketched a magic circle in the dirt floor around us. "Come, friends," he said. "Invoke the God-dess with me. Either this Lancelot/Gwenevere madness will end or Arthur's Peace will end. It is only a matter of time."

We three worked hard. We did our best. But when we returned to the forest six moons later, the Lancelot/Gwenevere madness still flowed in full flood.

6
HISTORY

For years Merlin, Aefa and I traveled to the kingdom when needed. Sometimes we spent moons there, sometimes days. Mellias, Lugh's groom, sometimes returned with us to the forest. Lugh—Lancelot—never did. Whenever I came home to the villa the Lady would look past me, wanting to see Lugh. But this was a want, not a hope. She knew he would never come back.

Slowly, I began to enjoy the kingdom. As experience softened the sharp edge of fear, I almost enjoyed the adventure of travel. Riding in open country I always dressed as a boy. Once in a while a canny Human would look down at me from his charger, or up at me as I sat my pony, and cross his fingers between us. Then I would laugh inside myself for sheer, delicious glee. The Humans' evil God Satan worked as my ally, though we never met.

Within Arthur's dun, I basked in the deep respect his jostling Human herd accorded me. Giants stood aside to let me pass; bright-gowned ladies hushed their chatter at my approach—this although I lived in Merlin's wicker hut under the rampart on bread, ale and wild greens. These folk who worshipped material things, whose true God was greed, yet feared my power.

Arthur deferred to me, though I lived under his hand, surrounded by knights who would lop off my head at his nod. Arthur treated me as courteously as he had in my forest, years ago. Naturally I had no care for Arthur. But I had not drowned my body with my heart in the Fey lake. Whenever I passed near Arthur, I remembered the white doe and the nightingale, and was conscious of my body's response.

Early in our travels, Merlin took me to Arimathea Monastery. That spring morning I felt a peace and serenity that reminded me almost of home. I relaxed slightly, noticing birds nesting on low branches and hares quiet in their forms. We rode toward the monastery, a circle of thatched huts, through blooming apple trees, fat, tended trees such as I had never seen. Clear notes of music dropped on us like rain as chapel bells warned the monks of our approach.

By Human standards, monks are not fearsome folk. Why should they be? They walk unarmed, threatening none. They keep few treasures in their huts that other Humans might covet. (And greed is usually the ground of Human violence.) Most Humans respect their spiritual power. (At least, the Angles I have known respect it. They say the Saxons are different.)

So no tense, armed men rushed from barns, huts or fields to confront us. Quiet men stepped through doors, downed tools, shaded their eyes and smiled at us (though I noticed a few sketched the sign in the air that my Human lover had sketched between us, five long years before).

These men walked gently and spoke softly, almost like Fey. When they moved into shadow I saw their auras, mild, peaceable colors, rippling like summer brooks. One or two had large white auras like Merlin's, or like the Lady's. Most of their auras told me that these men were celibate. Some of them were virgins. I thought they must learn great magic here—a monastery must be a school of magic, as the Children's Guard was a school of forest lore—for why would anyone remain celibate, if not to practice magic?

I dismounted slowly, glancing about uneasily—not apprehensive of the monks themselves, but of the aura of their powerful magic; and soon I felt it brush against us, a perceptible spiritual wind. Merlin saw me glance over my shoulder. He finger-signed, *It comes from the central hut.*

The chapel. I turned my mind there, and sure enough, that was the source of the wind. Steadily it blew from there, from the thatched roof, from the strange wooden figure that rose over the smoke hole: two . . . poles . . . crossed, one over the other. It reminded me of the Lady conversing with spirits, standing erect, arms and legs extended, inviting east and west to meet in her body.

On that first visit I did not go into the chapel. I did so on later visits, and so I came to see the carved wooden Gods and the everburning lamp; but inside the chapel the magic pooled like a deep lake with me at its bottom, and I never stayed there long.

We had come to Arimathea to see Merlin's old friend and schoolmate, Abbot Gildas.

Abbot Gildas was a small, lean man whose bushy red hair was salted with white. His red eyebrows twitched, bunched and stretched with every thought that flickered through his quick mind. Sitting cross-legged under his curving hut-wall, I could watch Gildas happily for hours as he listened to Merlin's songs, tales and poems, and answered with his own, all the time twitching or frowning, grinning or growling. I found him endlessly entertaining.

He sat at a table with parchment, quill and ink before him. Merlin sat on a stool beside him, Enchanter on his knee, and even when song was uncalled for, his even-length fingers wandered the strings. There was no moment of silence in Gildas' hut when we were there, but only talk, laughter, angry hisses, song, and Enchanter's rippling, tinkling comments.

I was the only silent being there; my part was to leap up at a small gesture from either Gildas or Merlin and run out to the cook-hut for more ale. Apart from this service I seemed to disappear and be forgotten, which well suited my Fey nature. I watched and listened like a Guard child in a tree, happy to receive, without giving, information.

I was known as Merlin's servant boy, Niv. Strangely, though we returned to Arimathea several times a year for fifteen years, Gildas never seemed to expect Niv to grow up. Niv remained the eternal child, useful for ale runs. Otherwise unconsidered.

Sometimes when Merlin told a story Gildas would bend over his parchment, dip his quill in ink and mark the parchment. Over several visits I observed this, growing more and more curious; finally one day I rose, stood at Gildas' shoulder and looked down at the ink marks. I must have thought myself truly invisible and beyond Gildas' observation.

Merlin said, "Niv, Gildas is writing a book."

I signed, *What?*

Merlin went on. "To those who can read, those ink marks speak. Monks yet unborn will read in Gildas' book of what happened in the kingdom before their time."

I signed, *Why?*

Gildas half-turned on his stool and looked up at me. The way his nostrils quivered, I saw that he had smelled as well as seen me. Quickly I skipped back. Gildas turned back. "Merlin, this boy should learn to read."

"You forget, friend. I have not that art myself."

"You should learn to read too!"

Merlin began to argue that reading might destroy his memory; Gildas produced feats of memory to disprove this theory; the two men argued, and Niv sank again into his invisible corner, glad to be forgotten.

Another time, Merlin sang for Gildas the Battle of Badon. Enchanter thrummed and drummed. Merlin's voice whispered and roared. He did not notice—but I did—how Gildas' brows and beard twitched, how his eyes flashed and his gnarled hands flexed.

Merlin had just reached the climax, where Arthur kills nine hundred Saxons with his magic sword Caliburn, when Gildas leapt up and shouted, "Sing me no more of this Arthur!"

Merlin looked up at him. Enchanter twanged once more and was silent. In excessively mild tones, Merlin remarked, "I have noted before now in this hut a certain lack of enthusiasm for the King. But you must write of him in your book. Arthur will be our history."

"Not in my book!" Gildas cried. "That cursed name is not mentioned in my book!"

"Hm," said Merlin. "And after all the tales I have told you! All that breath wasted . . ." As if absently he caressed Enchanter, and sweet notes drowned out Gildas' harsh breathing. "This is because of your brother, I suppose. Whom Arthur killed."

"No! My brigand brother deserved his fate!"

"Well. I am glad to see you so fair-minded. But why, then—"

"You know how Arthur paid for that Badon battle! And all the other battles!"

"Paid for . . . ? I never thought about it."

Neither had I. Even now, after all my experience with Humans, I am still surprised by greed, and the vast importance of pence and gold in Human affairs. Very few Humans will take a step that does not enrich them. I know this but tend to forget it because it seems so unnatural to me. In the case of war, for instance, I would suppose men would fight for their lives, homes and freedom without being paid. I would suppose that chargers and swords and shields and lives would be given freely. But no; men will fight freely when the enemy stands at their door, but not when he waits in the next village.

Abbott Gildas enlightened us as to Arthur's means of funding his militia. "He robbed the monasteries, brother!"

"Ah." Merlin stroked his beard. "You monks take a vow of poverty, am I wrong?"

"Don't be a child! Niv over there knows monks have to eat!"

"And drink good ale." Merlin nodded.

"And keep the tapers burning in the chapel! And keep decently clothed!"

"So for this you leave Arthur out of history?' "

"What other revenge can I take?"

Merlin smiled. "You surprise me, Gildas, seeking revenge!"

"Well. I am only Human."

"But you will find it hard to leave Arthur out entirely. You will have little history left."

"What little I have will be a moral history!"

"But consider, friend Gildas; Arthur—"

"Do not name him again to me!"

"—The King, by fighting back Saxons, allows your monastery to flourish. Yours and all the others. Your Christian church grows like a vine in his shadow. Without his sword Caliburn in their way, the Saxons would have hung you on a tree for Odin by now."

Gildas twitched his brows and muttered, and finally changed the subject.

As we rode away, I suggested to Merlin, "Why do you not ask Gildas to teach you to write? There is power in that."

Merlin growled like a bothered bear. "We are not brothers, Gildas and I."

"He calls you so."

"We are old friends who followed the path of wisdom together since boyhood. But there comes a fork in that path where we part company. Niviene, have you noticed the sign that some of the brothers draw in the air when they see us?"

"The sign against evil."

"Ah, indeed! That is a sign against the 'Father of the Lies,' the 'Prince of Darkness,' the foul fiend himself!"

"In truth?"

"The brothers know I am half Fey and that I deal with the Fey, who are devils."

I felt again the familiar delight in power. "I did not know we were so dangerous! I am deeply flattered, Merlin!"

"If they knew you were Fey . . ." Merlin shuddered. "For that matter, if they knew you were female . . ."

96

"What would they do?"

"Well . . . I do not think they would harm us."

"You do not think so." Merlin's words sobered me. I felt now a prickling of unease.

"But they would certainly cast us out of their midst forever."

"Ah. Is that all?"

"And they would burn herbs in Gildas' hut to purify the air. And they might burn Gildas' book, though he is the Abbot."

"But they would not burn us."

"I cannot be sure of that."

So even Gildas and his brothers, who spoke softly and walked gently, almost like Fey, could turn and rend like the rest of their savage kind.

During another visit, Gildas spoke to enlighten me. "Chivalry," he said, "is the knights' rule of life. Monks have their rule to guide them in serving God. Knights have their rule to guide them in serving their chief. Or their duke. Or their king. A knight would no more offend his king than a monk would sin against God." Gildas' red eyebrows twitched. "How is it you are so ignorant of the world, Niv? Where have you been all your life?"

Merlin saved me from answering. He held out his mug for more ale and chuckled. "I have very cleverly combined chivalry with piety," he told Gildas happily.

Turning to Merlin, Gildas forgot me. "How do you mean?"

"You have heard tell of the Holy Grail."

Gildas paused, considering all the things of which he had heard. "Hah! The grail our Lord used at the Last Supper, in which He gave his followers the first Eucharist. Brought overseas to Britain by His disciple Joseph of Arimathea and Saint Mary Magdalene. What has all that to do with chivalry?"

Merlin grinned. "I have convinced the King to send forth his knights to find this Holy Grail. Thus I combine chivalry with piety and keep a horde of bloody-minded men busy in peacetime."

"Hah! Hmmm." Gildas knit his brows. "If they find the Grail, how will they know it? What does it look like?"

"As you might suppose, the Holy Grail is pure gold."

"Most unlikely!"

"Inlaid with scenes from the life of the Savior—"

"Pshaw!"

"—and guarded by angels whose heavenly song drives mad the unworthy seeker. Some knights have returned frothing-mad already."

Gildas threw his white head back, slapped his knees and laughed.

Why did he laugh? Madness was no joke. In truth, my brother Lugh was the only frothing madman I had ever seen, but I had no wish to see more.

Now and then, Lugh fell into wild rages in which he truly frothed, and cut about with his great sword, and reeled through the streets, roaring. Innocent Humans ran all over each other to get out of his way.

The first time I saw this I leaned out the door of our hut, wondering what to do. Mellias, scurrying after Lugh, made violent signs to me: *Stay away!* So I drew back into shadow and watched as Mellias deftly tripped Lugh so that Lugh fell flat, tossed Lugh's sword away, then knelt beside him, patting and murmuring. From a safe distance a Human crowd watched as Mellias helped Lugh up and led him gently away, one small arm halfway around Lugh's waist.

Beside me, Merlin said, "That is Lugh, you know."

I stared at him.

He stroked his beard. "The knight, honored by all, is Lancelot."

"Yes."

"But Lugh lives inside Lancelot, asleep. Forgotten."

"Ah." I began to see.

"Now and then, Lugh wakes up, confused. Angry, because he has to sleep his life away."

Dull sorrow pressed my chin down to my breastbone.

So why did Gildas laugh? Maybe he knew Merlin was lying about the frothing-mad grail hunters. They made a grand story, such as Merlin loved to sing, but there was no truth in it.

Maybe Gildas was heartless, like me. He thought so little of so many folk!

A Merlin Song

Who are those men who ride so fast
Early and late, first light and last,
Searching each farm and town and village,
Like enemies in search of pillage,
And slow their ponies' frantic paces
Only to look at children's faces?

King Vortigern, the Saxon's friend,
Seeks his crumbled fort to mend.

How shall these hunters mend a fort?
They hunt not meat, nor pause for sport,
They slow their ponies' frantic paces
Only to look at children's faces.
How shall these hunters mend a fort?
What word will they take to Vortigern's court?
King Vortigern, the Saxon's friend,
To his fort's crumbling seeks an end.
Three times the new-built fort has crumbled.
Three times its battlements have tumbled.
Three times his druid priest has mumbled,
"Seek the child.
Find the child.
Bring the child.
Slay the child.
Mix with your mortar the blood of the child
Whose father's unknown, from hell or the wild."

Therefore the hunters ride so fast
Early and late, first light and last,

Slowing their ponies' frantic paces
Only to look at children's faces.

The child-hunters homeward turn,
Back to the land of Vortigern.
Whose child does the leader carry before him?
What unhappy mother bore him?

Child of the father from hell or the wild,
Child of the Fey, a herd-maid's child.
Leaving her folk, she has gone for a nun
To pray for the soul of her little son.
His blood will mix with Vortigern's mortar.
Then Vortigern's tower will guard his border.

How fast they ride away from the light
Into the shade of nearing night!
They sought the child
They found the child.
They took the child,
They'll slay the child—
Willingly bear they dread and fear
At the word of a bloody druid seer . . .

7

MORGAN'S DOOR

Fifteen years after this conversation, as we stood before Morgan le Faye's door, I wondered what Gildas and his brothers thought of *her*! And what steps they might take against her, were she not Arthur's half-sister. And I wondered if she were named in Gildas' moral history.

In the far north of Arthur's realm you leave villages and duns behind. You ride through open country, barren but for patches of gorse and heather, where, even in sunshine, wind moans among rocks. Ravens and falcons sweep the sky in ominous patterns. Small herds of red deer flow over distant hills. The nearest village is a day's ride south.

Rain spattered that spring morning. Our tired ponies cropped the moor behind us. Before us rose Morgan's Mount, a small, rounded hill of the kind druids say were man-built in ancient times. Humans have been shifting earth for a long, long time. Earthworking must be natural to them, as it is to ants.

Morgan's door was easily found, an old, battered wooden door, moldy, curtained in green-budding vines. Its iron latch was rusted through. It looked as though the whole door would crumble at a push. Behind that door, under the hill, Morgan le Fey awaited us, Arthur's half-sister, the Witch Queen.

Behind that door and under the hill Caliburn awaited us—Caliburn, who had hung over Arthur's high seat together with his Goddess shield till Morgan stole the sword.

Who but Morgan le Faye would dream to dare to steal Caliburn? Caliburn was magic. Caliburn was . . . sacred.

When Arthur found Caliburn gone from the wall over his high seat along with visiting Morgan, he first hastened to cover the theft. Another sword, quickly hung beside the Goddess shield, passed for Caliburn. While the Angles thought Caliburn safe above Arthur's high seat, his crown was secure.

Next he called for Merlin. His messengers scouted the eight directions, asking for Merlin at taverns, monasteries, Druid schools, noble manors, chiefs' duns. But no messenger found Merlin. The mage himself scried Arthur's need in the Fey lake waters; so we came to Arthur out of the Fey forest. From Apple Island and Lady Villa, Merlin, Aefa and I rode out yet one more time through an icy spring rain into the dangerous kingdom.

Now the sun rose, a vague shimmer through rain-mist, and Merlin squared his thin shoulders. Now was the time to confront the witch, while the sun looked down. Not even Merlin had wanted to push that crumbling door open during the night.

I glanced at my companions.

Armed with spear, cuirass and helmet, my brother Lugh crouched before the door.

In twenty years, Lugh had, in essence, turned Human. Even fifteen years before, seeing him again, I had not known him. I had seen a giant knight like any other lumber toward me, and pause. They often paused, then took a cautious detour by me. But this knight raised astonished hands. Surprise lit his face, and he blushed. "Niviene!" he roared. "Sister!" And he marched up and embraced me with iron arms.

"Lugh!"

"Lancelot," he whispered into my ear. "Remember: Lancelot."

He insisted I call him that, though to this day I still forgot. He never asked after the Lady, our mother; he never mentioned our childhood, our home, our memories. Lancelot and Lugh were two separate beings; and Merlin said that only one of them could live under the sun at a time. For now, it was Lancelot's turn. So it was then; and fifteen years later Lugh's only protest was the wild rage that sometimes overwhelmed Lancelot. When Mellias saw that one of these rages approached, he would lead Lancelot out of the dun to some secret place, sometimes to stay hidden for moons at a time.

Mellias, known to Humans as Lancelot's servant Mell, was no longer deaf and dumb. Yet he was known to have "something wrong somewhere." This caused no comment. Very many Humans have "something wrong somewhere." Mellias was wholly Fey. Often he came home to the forest—as I did myself—to fish and dance, and to court me, smiling. (I withheld myself from Mellias and all others for the sake of my power. Yet always, under boy's shirt or lady's gown, I wore Mellias' stolen crystal, swinging on its thong.) After a while he would return again to be Lancelot's faithful Mell, to grease his harness and groom his charger. Mellias loved adventure. And he seemed to love Lancelot.

Now Mellias smiled at me over Lugh's head. He and Lugh knew no magic. They were not here to war on the witch, but to guard against brigands, Saxons and Picts. Yet Mellias alone seemed to have no fear of Morgan. Clear in my head I heard his thought: *If this Morgan is a woman, I can tame her!*

Aefa cocked her head and fixed keen eyes on Morgan's door as though it were an ordinary door that she could "see through." But this door was magically sealed, and none of us could guess what might lie behind it. Witch Morgan might lean against it herself, listening to our breathing and to our ponies' teeth cropping grass.

Ravens called warning, sweeping widdershins over us, and Merlin glanced up to check the pattern of their flight.

Years had bowed Merlin and silvered his hair and beard. Wrinkles mapped his lean face. Wrapped in his shabby homespun cloak he might have been any Human oldster, looking to lay down his bones to the Goddess, but for the snap and sparkle of his grey eyes—which he veiled, for Humans—and the silver mist of his aura, which Humans could not see.

He it was who scried in fire that Morgan was indeed the sword-stealer. He it was who led us, by the stars and his bending wand, to her hill. When we came to the last village, a day's ride behind us now, her peasants pointed the way wordless, fingers crossed. They feared their witch, but they knew of Merlin and feared him more.

Now we sat hunched in thought before Morgan's door. Lugh turned to inspect the wide, rainy landscape. Aefa and I watched Merlin.

He brightened, scurried away to the pack pony and brought back a skin-wrapped package: the harp Enchanter. I hand-signaled, *Witch Morgan has heard music before.* Merlin shrugged. *Not Enchanter's music!*

While tuning Enchanter in the rain he sent us each a glance and each remembered a time when Enchanter had shown his power. Lugh and the Otter may have remembered a night in Lady Villa, twenty years gone. Aefa and I had seen whole roistering taverns magicked to silence. On one particularly dangerous occasion, Enchanter had cast all listeners into a deep sleep, during which we Fey slipped safely away.

"Where's Otter?" Merlin had abandoned his tuning and was looking around. The battered, moldy door behind the vines stood open. Mellias was gone.

I whirled on Lugh. "You let him go!"

Lugh shrugged. "The door was only sealed against magic. It opened at a touch."

"He came along to help you guard the door, not to face the witch alone!"

"How would you have had me stop him?"

The Fey do not impose their will. But with Lugh . . . "With you I never know if I am dealing with Human or Fey."

A bitter smile creased Lugh's grey eyes. "Neither do I."

Merlin whispered, "Enough talk! Let us go!"

I touched Mellias' crystal. It warmed my fingers as I slipped after him through Morgan's cracked-open door.

One step inside, I found myself in complete darkness. I smelled Aefa at my elbow, Merlin some way back, and some cold, vegetative smell. I heard Merlin hiss, "Hold still!"

Something slithered across my foot. Aefa breathed, "Adders."

As my Fey eyes adjusted, darkness turned dim and I saw movement around our feet. Adders surrounded us, wriggling, rearing, slipping across and over each other. Now I could even see their tongues darting in and out, testing our smell. Aefa said aloud, "Pretty ones! Children of the Goddess, make way for us."

Rising, the snakes swayed knee-high. From childhood experiments I knew they could not hear us, but Aefa's voice had set the stale air moving.

Merlin raised his voice in song. The small, dangerous heads turned in his direction; the curious tongues lunged out.

Aefa and I sang with Merlin. As our voices shook the air, one by one the snakes lowered, turned away, flowed away.

Merlin paused to ask, "Are they gone?" I remembered, then, that his eyes were only half Fey; he could barely see in the darkness. "Going," I told him. I sang to the last few, *One bite of us will poison you.*

Aefa said, "Gone."

"Then move forward, slowly," Merlin ordered. "Niviene first. Aefa, hold my hand. Gods, I can't see beyond a step!"

We moved forward.

Soft cobwebs brushed our faces. The passage narrowed till we could touch both walls and had to stoop under the rough stone roof, with Merlin bent double. I thought, This cannot be Morgan's own entrance. She must have another, hidden door.

107

Aefa whispered, "Cold down here!"

"Either it's cold or I am craven."

We edged forward into heavy cold, a pool of spiritual winter, such as I remembered feeling before. But that time I had sought it deliberately. I said, "Aefa, I think—"

A kilted giant warrior stepped out of the wall ahead. He lifted one booted foot free of the wall, and then the other, and hefted his javelin. Aefa gasped.

The warrior shone of his own light like a star in the night sky, so Merlin saw him as clearly as we did. He growled, "Ghost, Aefa. Only a ghost."

Beside me, Aefa stiffened. Spirit conversation was no talent of hers.

The warrior hurled his ghost javelin cleanly through my neck. Icicle-cold, it sliced through me and melted.

Crouched under the roof, I lowered my head like a bull and charged the giant. My head and shoulders burst through his icy form and I rushed clear, hearing his disappointed roar inside my ears.

I stopped to look back. The giant form dissolved into a shining mist through which Aefa led Merlin by the hand.

"The druids are right," he declared, stumbling. "These man-built hills are tombs of the Old Ones. They sacrificed that man to guard the passage; and still he stays on, though he has long been spirit. Niviene, lead on."

Shuffling slowly down the sloping passage, I sent my spirit ahead to spy.

I had never met or seen Witch Morgan. What might she be like? I knew only that she was Arthur's half-sister, reputedly wise and wicked. Why had she stolen Caliburn from Arthur's hall? And what did it matter? Did Arthur's Peace truly depend on the magic sword? And if it did, did the safety of our forest truly depend on Arthur's Peace?

Merlin whispered, "Niviene, why have you stopped?"

"I was thinking, Merlin; wondering why we are creeping down into this trap."

"Hah!"

"Morgan might turn us all into snakes."

(Once I had asked the Lady, "Can magic turn man into bat?" She had told me, "Spirit, once shaped in flesh, holds that shape. But a clever mage can make a man think he is a bat.")

"Hah!" Merlin almost spat. "She's turned you into a coward, anyhow!"

And I saw that this was true. My spirit, scouting ahead, had met Morgan's spirit; and she had sent me frightened, doubting thoughts.

"Move!" Merlin commanded. "Lead! Think no more, just walk!"

I obeyed. Moments later, a dim light swam before us.

We stopped and bunched together, like three white deer I had seen lately under Counsel Oak. The deer had stamped and jostled and gazed at me over each other's shoulders, ears and tails a-twitch. So we three now gazed and shifted and sought each other's hands.

Ahead, the faint light shimmered, dimmed and strengthened. Merlin muttered, "It's reflected. See? Off the wall." He was right. The tunnel took a turn, there. The light shone from beyond the turn.

The three white deer under Counsel Oak had leaped apart in three directions and vanished in shadow. We three crept forward like one three-headed monster and turned the corner.

❧

Tristam played his harp at Yseult's feet. She leaned forward in her seat and smiled. Behind her, dagger upraised, King Mark rose up out of gloom.

The tapestry glowed, the figures almost moved, in the light of a bronze lamp set on the floor. Other tapestries covered the round wall of the small room, each one lit by its own bronze lamp. One

109

showed the Holy Grail, a golden dish borne aloft by winged spirits. One showed Arthur, knee deep in lake water, taking Caliburn from the Lady's hand.

No rushes matted the floor, but rather a green and blue carpet stitched with intricate designs. In the center stood a heavy, round table; and facing us across this table, young Arthur sat over a chess board.

This was almost the man who once chased a white doe into an enchanted forest. My heart leapt like an unborn child at sight of him.

Then I saw that he was younger, slighter, and that his aura, dim in the lamp light, was a sickening grey laced with black.

Mellias, his back turned to us, leaned over the table.

"Arthur" looked up at us and leered.

In two strides I was at Mellias' side. "Mellias!" He never stirred. He was frozen, leaning on his hands on the table; he might have been carved from wood. His eyes were glazed.

"Arthur" turned back to the game. His fingers, even-lengthened like my own, reaching for a black queen on the chess board, hinted at power; but I felt a much larger power nearby, compared to which "Arthur" was a mere decoy, like a wooden duck floating near a hunter's blind.

Merlin and Aefa moved up beside me. Merlin growled, "We have come from far off to speak with the Lady Morgan."

Grinning up at Merlin, "Arthur" touched the black queen. Now I wished I had learned chess when Merlin had offered to teach me. Then I could have read the message laid out on this board. I knew enough to recognize the white king and abbot, in line with the black queen.

Merlin betrayed impatience. Merlin was old, now. He had ridden hard for days, and camped in the rain outside Morgan's door. He was through with games, hints, mental duels.

Like a hound that tracks otter and ignores the hare in his path, he prepared to charge straight through "Arthur" to Morgan, his quarry. Black anger flared in his aura. His brows and beard twisted, he pointed a knob-boned finger at "Arthur."

"Arthur" swept the black queen across the board and knocked the white abbot off.

Merlin drew breath to curse. I touched his elbow.

Large shadows swooped around the wall like bats. Like a smell, a perception pervaded the room. It tightened skin and shortened breath.

Aefa gasped and turned a slow, dizzy circle. I reeled and leaned on the table beside Mellias.

"Arthur's" grey eyes smiled at me, like the King's eyes when he first saw me come through his hall, past his giants and hounds. "Arthur" leaned back and folded his arms—the King's very gesture.

Then he diminished. His grey aura flickered and dimmed as the perceived power drew near.

Aefa drew her knife, and fainted on the carpet.

I was going to be sick.

Quickly I gathered my spirit and sent it up through my head to sit in air just under the ceiling, a drifting mist of consciousness apart from my body. Merlin was up there with me; I heard him think, *Just in time, Niviene.*

Free now of physical sensations I came fully alive to every breath of underground air. I expanded my consciousness to fill the small room. Another consciousness pulsed in and out of my own, dark, gloating, confident of victory. I felt it laugh without mirth.

The Holy Grail tapestry trembled; shook, tightened, lifted. Light flowed from behind it; and in the light stood a tall, graceful figure, one hand holding back the tapestry, the other wielding a wand.

Morgan le Faye stepped into the room. The tapestry dropped back in place behind her.

She wore a gold torque at her throat, a black tunic and white overgown; neck, ears, loose black hair, wrists, brow and nostril were studded with gleaming gems. Her aura was a huge silver mist matching Merlin's, that stretched halfway round the room. Its edges burst into happy little flames. Already, Morgan regarded us as her prisoners.

She nodded merrily to Merlin and spoke to him in Latin. I tried vainly to read her mind. It was closed to me, sealed tighter than her door.

In Angle, Merlin answered her:

"Why have you done this, Morgan le Faye?
Why have you stolen your brother's prize?
Arthur's Peace has made you wealthy.
Arthur should be as a pearl in your eyes."

Laughingly, Morgan replied,

"Before he was born, he was my foe.
Well I remember that night of woe.
Why did you carry the child away,
Whom Uther sought, at break of day?"

Merlin said,

"He could not know the child his own,
Conceived before Gorlois' death was known."

And Morgan:

"A good thing, that! Why did you meddle?"

Merlin:

"I knew that child had kingly mettle,
And would not let the Saxons settle.
He needed but raising, humble and hidden;
He would come forth to rule when he was bidden."

Morgan:

"By you, of course! The wise king-maker!"

Merlin:

"Not to be thwarted by a sword-taker."

Morgan laughed.

"What have the Saxons done to me?
But Arthur! That you plainly see.
He came from nowhere, humble and hidden,
Drew sword from stone, as he was bidden.
He drove the Saxons from the land,
Then in my country took his stand.
Now I dwell under my magic hill,
Where old bones lie and ghosts roam still,
While Arthur feasts in my banquet hall,
And you feast beside his earthen wall."

Merlin lowered his staff slightly. In an almost plaintive voice, he said.

"Lest the Saxons fall on the innocent,
On rape and pillage and murder bent,
Leave Caliburn in Arthur's hand.
Let him defend your peoples' land."

Morgan:

"The innocent? Now who are they?"

Merlin:

"Those who follow the Goddess' way,
Planting and harvesting, doing no harm—"

Morgan:

"There is no innocent under the sky
Save maybe the grass that lives to die
So man and beast can live and feast!
If there were innocence found in man
—As there has not been since the race began—
You yourself would innocent be,
For folly and innocence brothers be.
You came for the sake of your precious lord,
Thinking to save him his famous sword."

Morgan's sneer would have frozen my blood, had I sat in my body.

"Enough of this talk! Merlin, be mouse!
Squeak and skitter through my house!"

Saying this, Morgan swept her glowing wand in a circle. Sparks flew at Merlin and glowed momentarily in his white hair and beard and on his homespun cloak. She stepped forward to strike him with the wand, but Merlin and I together raised a shield of power before him.

Never had I felt so threatened. For the first time in my life I saw Merlin as possibly vincible. If Morgan broke the shield and touched him, I thought she might truly send him skittering and squeaking away like a mouse. I had never before come up against such power as hers.

Morgan stopped, baffled by our shield. She could not know that we were using all our combined power to hold it in place. I felt as though I were holding a heavy shield up in both hands; my body, below me, broke out in actual sweat.

114

For the first time she noticed me.

"Aha!" She murmured, frowning. "And who is this boy, this child you have brought to defend you? He will make a good servant when I have tamed him."

Merlin managed to answer, though his voice trembled. "You know better than that, Morgan."

I felt his power sinking away. He could make no further effort.

Morgan purred, "I suppose this is your consort, Niviene, famous at my brother's court. And this is why you are now my captive; for this mistress of yours has drained your power."

I said courteously, "You are mistaken, Witch Morgan. At your brother's court I am known as Virgin Niviene. You did not know that?"

She did not. Her grey eyes, so like Arthur's, widened briefly. I smiled at her, open-mouthed.

She actually drew back a step. We felt the air lighten, and Morgan's power withdraw, as a serpent withdraws the better to strike. She said, "You are Fey."

In the moment of her withdrawal, Merlin and I swooped down into our bodies. Now we were subject to sweat and trembling and nausea, but the effort of holding the shield was easier with this leverage.

I tried to hold Morgan's attention. "I am Fey like you, Morgan."

"No, no. I am Human. My father was Duke Gorlois, Lady Ygraine's husband."

"Are you sure of that?" I grinned widely. "Who can be sure of her father? Merlin magicked Ygraine so that she thought Uther her husband, so we are told. Could not a Fey magician have done the same and slept with her himself? The lady cannot have been very wise."

Now I had her attention! She leaned forward, her wand drooped toward the floor. I was delighted to see anger in her face.

"That is a lie!" she cried. "Merlin's lie!"

From the corner of my eye, I saw the young man at the table stir. "Mother," he murmured, "Mother, calm—"

She snapped her wand at him and he fell silent.

Witch Morgan had given way to passion. Anger ruled her. We felt her power ebbing from all around the room, like an out-flowing tide, as anger consumed its energy. Just as I was catching my first easy breath, I felt the pressure of her force double. I sank to my knees, perplexed, barely holding the shield intact. Whence came the sudden force? Not from the witch. It was almost as if . . . as if . . .

Merlin had let go.

I heard a familiar sound from beside me . . . music? . . . just before I fainted.

I came to, apparently seconds later. Music filled the room, the notes falling like blessed raindrops on a parched field, leaving no space for thought, feeling or action outside itself. Morgan's wand-tip was sinking toward the floor. Her son sat tranced, soft mouth hanging open.

Merlin was singing of a dun under siege, a different tale from that he usually sang to the world outside . . . The red and black pennants snapped in the wind, While Uther stared fixedly at Gorlois' dun. Little cared he for the booty within. His men dreamed of gold, enamel and cloth; Uther dreamed only of Gorlois' wife.

Inside paced the lady, who wrung her hands; She feared for her safety, and that of her girls. Crouched by the wall behind tapestries, The girls watched their mother pace and ponder.

Two children sick with bewildered fright. Hearing the shouting, horn-blowing and hoof-thunder. Morgan felt strongly her mother's fear. She watched Ygraine sweep back and forth, Hands twisting together like mating snakes. Morgan twisted her sister's hand likewise.

Merlin sang all this as though he had hidden behind the tapestry himself. Witch Morgan leaned against the wall, grey eyes wide with remembrance, brimming with tears.

Small Morgan wanted the uproar gone. She wanted her mother's arms around her. She wanted her corn-doll, who lay far away; In the rushes it lay, near Ygraine's foot. Ygraine swung away; her back was turned; Little Morgan darted out to snatch up the doll.

A giant burst open the chamber doors. Morgan stared up his massive length. His tunic crawled with red and black dragons, Each one larger than Morgan's whole. In one mailed hand gripped he a naked sword, Bloody tip eye-to-eye with the child. The other hand shot out and grabbed her braid. Ygraine swung about, saw, cried out.

Listening, Morgan cried out. Frost-pale, she dropped her wand. Her son rose from his seat.

Before he could move I ran to Morgan, seized her loose black hair in one hand and drew my knife with the other.

This stopped the son in his tracks. Morgan's grey eyes snapped back to life, snapped fire. Half-hypnotized, she struggled to surface, to regain control. But my hold was firm, and the battle was ended.

Almost as if rubbing salt in the wound, Merlin never missed a beat. He sang, damp harp strings slipping out of tune, of Uther's advance upon Ygraine.

Uther let go of Morgan le Faye. He sheathed his sword with a screech and a clank. Backing Ygraine against a table; He tore her skirt as she started to scream. Morgan tried to run back to her sister; But the concealing tapestry was too far. Her small legs fright-weakened, her knees a-tremble, She sank down on the rushes and sobbed.

So did Lady Morgan sink to her rich carpet, head hung: I sank with her, knife to throat.

Merlin swept the harp strings roundly and slung Enchanter back over his shoulder. His work was done.

Had I a heart I would have been undone as Morgan by this terrible tale. I later wondered why the Goddess allows the race of Humans to sully her earth. Their savagery, I thought, was matched only by that of spider and mantis.

At the moment, my concern was before me; but, between her memories and her defeat, Morgan was lost. She leaned against the wall, eyes glazed, no threat to us now—or to Arthur's Peace. I rose and stood back, sheathing my knife.

Merlin nodded to "Arthur." Silently obedient, the young man left the room by way of the Grail tapestry.

Next, Merlin turned to Aefa and helped her to her feet. She leaned dizzily on the table while Merlin waked Mellias from his trance with three hand-passes. Mellias whipped out his knife, looked around, saw the vanquished Morgan and sheathed it.

Back through the Grail tapestry came young "Arthur," bearing in both small, even-fingered hands a dark-sheathed sword which he laid on the table before Merlin. The mage drew the sword from its sheath. The blade shone like lightning. Ogham writing engraved on the blade flamed its message around the room. Merlin nodded.

"Ah," he breathed. "Caliburn himself." And he bowed to the sword, and said to us, "Children, look well. You may never see Caliburn shine like this again."

But I was looking at the young man, Morgan's son. He was beautiful, young Arthur without the driving energy. (Arthur would have grabbed Merlin by his stringy throat before ever a note was sung.) As I scanned his dark face and averted eyes, a nightingale seemed to trill in a far forest.

I probed his mind. Entering easily, I drifted in mist with an indoor, underground feeling. Uneasily I sought a door. I found one, drifting up against it in the soupy mist, but I could not open it. It was made of . . . iron, and barred shut. I could neither open it nor float through it; it was more closely sealed than the door to Morgan's Hill. Whatever hid behind that door would hide forever. And there, I thought, hid the real man, the wellsprings of him, his past, his truth, forever beyond my reach—and his.

I turned away. A light flickered, the mist parted, and I saw Caliburn shine in my mother's hand raised above the water. And Arthur—our real, grey-haired Arthur—took Caliburn from the Lady's hand, and turned, and handed him to . . . Morgan's son. Arthur's nephew. Whose name, I knew now, was Mordred.

And there stood Witch Morgan on an edge of light, a shadow but for her gleaming, reflecting jewels; torque, bracelets, pendants, rings and the gold-worked hem of her gown.

Morgan had taught her son this vision of Arthur, Caliburn and himself. This was her mother-gift to him.

I came back gratefully to outer reality to hear Merlin say, "Morgan, your son will come with us as Arthur's hostage."

Mordred's dark lashes fluttered in surprise. He backed slowly away, edging around the table. But Morgan answered flatly, "So be it. Mordred should meet his uncle."

And Mordred stood still as a puppet hung from a stick that passes from hand to hand. I did not want to move again into that dark mind and know its thoughts. I shook his spiritual touch off me like dried mud. But I knew I did not care to ride all the way back to Arthur's dun with this beautiful, rotten young man. Guarding him—and ourselves from him—would require endless wakefulness.

Morgan and Mordred exchanged a long, deep glance. Her gaze unfaltering, she continued, "The High King is Mordred's uncle, you know."

I felt like a wild-animal trainer I once saw at Arthur's court, standing between bear and wolf, armed only with a short whip.

8

MIDSUMMER NIGHT

⚜

Midsummer Night; Flowering Moon.

As on many a night, I walked the rampart above the dun. Humans being more unpredictable than bears, I preferred to watch them from a distance. The rampart allowed me to walk unimpeded and breathe free air, as I could not do in our wicker hut. And up here I could think without interruption.

Under a dark moon I met ghosts up here. Warriors from ancient times drifted in my path, for Arthur's dun was built upon an older one. Skin-clad women cradled scrawny babies. Weird animals lumbered in air: immense hogs with long, swinging noses; enormous, dagger-toothed cats. I was not sure if these were thought-forms created in song and story down in the dun or true spirits.

But tonight was magic. After a heady day's celebration the dun still buzzed and hummed. Fires bloomed on street corners. Giants laughed and gamed and fought, children ran and shouted. The noise drove my thoughts in dizzy circles.

Tonight the moon flowered. Clearer than the mumbling roar of the dun I almost heard distant pipes, distant drums. My walk bounced and skipped and slipped into dance.

Close ahead, a voice chuckled. Utterly startled, I moved no muscle, but studied the rampart ahead. A man was wrapped in an "invisible" hooded mantle.

He blocked my path, feet planted wide, arms folded under his mantle. "God's blood!" he said merrily, "Mage Niviene spies on my dun by moonlight!"

I murmured, "My Lord."

He tossed back his hood so my Fey eyes could search his face. "Walk with me," he commanded, smiling. And he turned to allow me to step beside him.

Side-by-side we swung along the narrow rampart ridge. Arthur smelled mildly of leather, sweat and gentle lust. Glancing up sideways, I saw pride in his large face, gazing down past me at King's Hall.

He said, "You did good work for me last spring, bringing Caliburn home."

"I fear we did you a disservice, too."

"You mean Mordred," Arthur said instantly. "I can handle Mordred."

"My Lord, he has great plans for himself."

Arthur chuckled.

I tried a nearer approach. "Mordred goes about now stirring your knights up . . ."

"Against me?"

"Not yet. But he rouses interest in what has been more or less secret."

"Not secret, Niviene. Unregarded."

We strolled above Queen's Hall. It came to me that if Lugh slipped into Queen's Hall in high moonlight we might see him. Maybe that was Arthur's intention here tonight.

Past the hall, he said, "Mordred has great plans?"

"I know he has."

"You have seen them in his mind!" Arthur teased.

Quietly, I assented. "Yes, I have."

"And do you see the great plans in my mind?" He stopped, took my chin in his left hand and tilted my face to his. "Show me your skill, Mage! Read my mind."

By moonlight a Human would have seen only darkness in his eyes. I saw humor, pride and . . . affection. (For me?) I sank easily into his mind and heart and read him, as he asked. I said, "You have held back the Saxons and preserved your kingdom. Now you mean to enlarge it."

"And then?"

"You mean to invade another people . . . I cannot quite see . . ."

"The Romans!" Excitement edged his voice.

The Romans were the folk who built Lady Villa, and other villas and towns. The Latin we were speaking was their language. That was all the Romans meant to me. But in Arthur's mind they represented supreme power and glory. Conquest of the Romans and their eternal city, Rome, would make him king of the world.

"And then . . . you want to create a new age . . . change the world . . ."

"I intend a golden age such as has never been seen on earth."

". . . Swords into plows . . ."

"Wars will end."

"Virgins . . . hung with jewels . . ."

"In my kingdom a virgin wearing a golden crown will be able to carry a golden grail to Hadrian's Wall, and no man will touch her!"

I said firmly, "That will never be." I had seen too much of Human nature.

Arthur laughed. "What I say will be, will be. They said the Saxons were here to stay. But I myself killed nine hundred of them in a day!"

"With the Goddess' help, remember." Though I had never yet understood that.

"What?" Arthur's hand dropped from my chin. "What Goddess helped me?"

"She who is painted on your shield."

"God's wounds, Niviene, no Goddess is painted on my shield!" It seemed I had insulted him. "That painting shows God's holy mother Mary!"

"In truth." As I had said, a Goddess. I was glad to know she was not *the* Goddess, for I had long wondered why She would favor one of Her sons above another. But a Christian Goddess would favor Christian over pagan, for sure. Truly wanting to understand, I asked, "This Goddess' child will grow up and be crucified?"

"Yes."

I wondered aloud, "Why could His holy mother not prevent that?"

Under the Flowering Moon I saw Arthur's eyes change. I felt his aura tingle, burn and expand. The giant standing over me seemed to grow immense wings, like the spirits painted in Christian chapels; and I thought, "Gods, he has risen into spirit!"

I rose in spirit myself and joined him.

We walked the sky, halfway to the Flowering Moon. Far below us, two statue-quiet figures faced one another on a high earth rampart. Below them on one side stretched earth, Goddess-lovely, clothed in silver night; on the other side Human bodies walked, made love, fought, ate or slept; Human spirits hovered like shining bees over clover, some in the flowers and some slightly above. A very few stood with us in the sky, like distant stars. The nearest of these I thought might be Merlin.

Beside me, Arthur shone like a star. His light eclipsed and embraced my own. Contemplating his mysterious religion, he had lost himself, and I saw no trace of pride, arrogance or ambition in the star he had become. I saw only the love I had glimpsed once before, lavished upon his land and his people, and now upon his Gods.

His star burned out quickly and he sank back into flesh. I followed him down.

He seemed unconscious of having gone anywhere else. He answered my question—Why could not His holy mother have prevented that—as though it had just left my lips. And maybe it had. Time passes differently in the spirit.

Arthur murmured, "And thine own heart a sword shall pierce."

"What?"

"A prophet told her that. A seer, like Merlin. She knew from the beginning that she would suffer. She sacrificed herself for the world."

I saw that he was thinking of the sacrifices he himself had made and would yet make, for his world. He added, "In the end a sword pierces every heart."

"Not mine!" I told him quickly. "No sword will pierce my heart ever again, for I have no heart."

Arthur looked down at me and laughed. Like a strong wind, his laughter blew away the shreds of solemn grandeur that had clung about him. He drew my hand under his arm and walked us along, free-striding. "I will let countless swords pierce mine," he said, "so I become king of the world, and bards will sing of me at a thousand hearths for a thousand years! History will remember me forever!"

"History?"

"Such history as monks write on parchment in dim cells, far from the roar of battle. But I suppose you know nothing of monks."

"I am not ignorant. I have met monks."

"And how did they greet you, Lady? I'll wager they thought you a temptation sent by Satan personally."

"They might have, my Lord, if I had not been disguised as a dirty, rough young boy."

Arthur's laughter startled a small herd of ponies feeding just below us. Snorting, the stallion trotted out of the rampart-shadow and looked fiercely about.

Intrigued, amused and incautious for once in my life, I said, "If you want history to remember you, rob no more monasteries."

Arthur stopped mid-stride. He swung me around to face him, and I looked up into a storm of rage. If I had been Human I would have sunk at his feet, cut down by sheer terror. Being Fey, I drew myself taller than ever before as he grabbed both my shoulders in fists suddenly turned iron.

Seduced by Arthur's high, rich spirit, warmed by his easy-seeming companionship, I had forgotten how Human he was. To a Human who wore a crown, spoke Latin and ate the grain of his own lands without labor, my words had been supremely insulting.

"Rob?" he roared down into my face. "Rob no more monasteries? When by God's bones and blood did I rob monasteries?"

His fists held me up. Below us, the stallion neighed louder than Arthur's shout and rushed away with his mares.

Arthur shook me as a woman shakes laundry. "What do you mean? When did I rob? By God's wounds, you will answer me!"

I could not. Shocked and fearful for my life, I yet could not speak to a Human who handled me so. Nature and training forbade.

Arthur's huge hands found my throat. His face had gone deadly pale, his eyes wild and wide. I prepared to rise into spirit for good.

His hands fell away. He gaped down at me, panting. Quickly, I stepped well back from him. He muttered, "Forgive me, Mage. I forgot who you were."

I made shift to nod. I had forgotten who he was, too.

"I heard the word 'rob,'" he went on. "Maybe you were joking?"

Out of reach I drew myself up very straight, tipped my head back and looked him in the eyes. I drew a hurting breath, cleared my throat and croaked, "Since you ask courteously, I will answer your question. You took monastery wealth to pay for the Battle of Badon. Therefore, a monk I know who writes history will not name you in his work."

Arthur breathed hard. "I see," he panted. "Would he have preferred to be abandoned to the Saxons? That was the choice."

I said nothing. He stepped toward me, I stepped back. He asked, "I suppose you will not reveal this fool of a monk's name."

"You suppose rightly."

He stepped toward me, I stepped back.

"Niviene," he whispered, and stopped. He cleared his throat and said clearly, "Niviene. I did not mean to touch you roughly."

"I believe you." I did.

"But I was meaning to touch you. I have meant to touch you now for . . . years. Have you wanted it, Niviene?"

"No."

"Did you not enjoy our first meeting?"

"I did . . . very much."

"Then . . ." I backed slowly before his slow advance.

"At our second meeting I told you I am given to magic—"

"I have respected that."

"Yes, you have."

"No Christian nun has received more respect from me."

Amazingly, even as I backed away, I was responding to him. How could I do that? This man had just choked me!

"Niviene, my doe . . ."

"No . . ."

"Walk with me. After twenty years, walk with me!"

I hesitated, and his arm came heavy and warm around me. I let him walk me off the rampart entirely and down the outer bank into the great summer meadow below. I let him press me down on earth's breast, shadowed from the moon under grass and flowers.

There I lost my power.

Greedily the Goddess sucked away my power, that I had stolen from Her.

Even as delight (almost forgotten except in dreams) over-whelmed me, I felt my power drain away into earth where it belonged, sinking like water into thirsty land.

For a while I could not think at all. The first thought that pierced my delicious confusion was, *Powerless, how shall I stop Mordred? I have left Merlin to fight Mordred alone.*

9

LAMMAS DAY

Lammas Day morning, bright-hot.

Basket on arm, I walked boldly around Queen's Hall and into Gwen's garden. Women with baskets wandered there, gathering herbs and chattering. One plunked a lute in the shade. As I came into the garden the lute fell silent. So did the women, mid-gossip.

I paused, looking for Gwen. Sunshine beat down on green and blue gowns and ribboned plaits. Round eyes and slack mouths stared at me. In my white gown under that sun, I must have shone like a Roman marble statue.

I felt my loss of power. I felt as Gwen must have felt in the Fey forest, years ago, lost in a land where she did not know the language, mind-misted.

Since I lay with Arthur in the meadow, auras had grown dim. I had learned to see auras even in brilliant sunshine, but now I could barely make out the grey mist of body-life around these women. Plants showed me no aura at all. Everything I saw was flat, as if

127

painted on a wall of air. No longer could I scry, in water or fire. I came here to Gwen's garden not because I had seen her here in our hearth-fire, but because I had overheard a conversation in the street. No longer could I enter a mind at will. Now mind-reading needed concentration, power fully focused. No longer could I smell minor emotion or intention. Only deep feeling—heavy lust, rage—reached my alert nose.

Never since childhood had I felt so vulnerable! I walked about in a mist of ignorance, guessing every step as Humans must. Humans lived like this always, from birth to death! My respect for them had decidedly increased. I had even learned some sympathy.

I saw Gwen. She knelt in a lavender patch, knife in hand, her back to all of us, blessedly alone. I glided up beside her, knelt, and planted my basket between us. Sometimes I wondered if love kept Gwen young, or if she drank a magic potion. Her bronze hair flowed free, held from her face by a silken ribbon. Her pale, freckled face and grey eyes were open and soft as a child's. Startled, she glanced at me sideways. And so warmly smiled that last day of summer that Gwen smiled back, almost forgetting her fear of me. Yet I needed no special power to guess her thought: *Again, this one! This small, dangerous person.* She could not imagine how far from dangerous I felt, how exposed. I felt I was going into battle naked and blindfolded.

We would not be alone for long. Women's voices rose again behind us, and the lute rippled. I leaned into the lavender as though cutting and whispered, "Beware the King."

Calmly, Gwen cut lavender. Softly she sang,

*"King Mark found Tristam and his lady sleeping
With Tristam's sword watch between them keeping."*

I returned,

*"He loved them both and so he stole away
And left them lying in the fading day."*

Then I added, "But no sword keeps watch between you and Lugh."

Gwen looked a question.

"Between you and Lancelot. Lady, the Angles blame you two for their poor harvests."

"Pagan folly!" Gwen tossed back her bright hair.

"And now comes hostage Mordred, murmuring of you to Arthur's knights! Gwen, Mordred's sly talk could crack the Round Table! On one side are Lugh's friends, on the other his enemies. And Arthur's Peace is forgotten. But you and Lugh—Lancelot— could yet sacrifice yourselves and mend the Round Table."

Gwen's freckled hands had paused among the lavenders. "What did you call me just now?"

Gods curse it, she had heard nothing I said! Her acorn-sized mind was too full of her own grandness. "Forgive me, I did not mean—"

"Viviene. What did you call me?"

I bit my tongue. When it hurt less I shrugged and admitted, "I called you Gwen, as once we all did."

"Who? Where? When?" Eagerly she leaned to me.

I had stumbled badly. There was no going back, but there might be defense. "When we were all young, in the Fey forest, where Mellias carried you off. You remember." I sat back on my heels and grinned at her, open-mouthed, filed canines on display.

Now Gwen might scream and shriek and have me driven from the garden like a weasel that had bit her. And like a weasel, I would have to streak for the nearest wood. Or she might seek—unwisely— to stab me with her lavender knife. Or she might sign the cross between us and cry for a priest.

Gwen crumbled. I guessed that she groped in her mind, grasping at dream-threads.

"God's blood!" she whispered. "I knew I had seen you before . . . You hid behind a bush and frightened me."

"It was you frightened me! I thought you were the Goddess."

"Mellias took me in there . . . He is Lancelot's groom, Mell, isn't he."

"Yes. See, you remember."

"And Merlin played his harp for us. Then I loved Lancelot, then and ever since."

I swung around to snarl at the women drawing near. They backed away as Gwen muttered, "God's blood! God's bones! God's holy mother! I never dreamed you were all Fey!" And she crossed herself.

I said firmly into her confusion, "Lady. Merlin and I have been keeping Mordred's power and influence in check, controlling the knights' responses. But now . . ." Now what? Now I have lain with your husband; Merlin, therefore, stands alone? ". . . Now I am powerless. But you and Lancelot together could mend the Round Table and save Arthur's Peace."

Gwen looked up at me so pale her freckles stood out like bruises. "Viviene, we all know that you are a virgin. You do not know what you ask." And, as she thought of what I asked, she gave forth the scents of rose and honeysuckle.

I warned her then. "Arthur will sacrifice you to his crown."

She dropped her eyes and nodded, slowly.

That was her decision. The Fey do not impose their will.

I rose and brushed earth from my gown. "Lady," I told her, "I am called Niviene. Not Viviene."

She nodded. "And I am called Your Majesty."

"I will remember that." Then I turned on my heel and left her and my empty basket among the lavenders.

❧

From Gwen's garden I went straight to find Lugh.

Lugh paid little heed to us mages in our wicker hut beneath the rampart. After our first joyful reunion, fifteen years before, he had ignored me as much as he could; he did not wish to be linked with us in the court mind. But he did send us messages through Mellias, who lived sometimes with us and sometimes in the stable.

I went now to the stable.

Immediately I was overwhelmed by the sweet, strong scent of new-mown hay. (It brought back powerful memories of childhood; of stealing into village barns with Elana and Lugh; of sleeping in hay, and slipping away in the dawn; of hiding stolen treasures in hay, some of which we forgot. The farmers must have puzzled over them later, as the winter hay supply shrank. "Well! Here's my adze! God's toes, how did it get here?")

On the last day of summer there were neither chargers nor donkeys nor ponies in the barn. They still pastured in the meadows beyond the rampart. Barn cats slunk and slept, mice rustled and crickets sang in the hay; Mellias' pipe sang too, away in a far corner behind hay stacks. It played "Yellow Leaves."

I drifted that way. The pipe paused and I called softly, "Lugh?"

I found Lugh and Otter Mellias cross-legged in the straw, a rough chess board and a skin of ale between them. Lugh must have been the only knight at Arthur's round table, or any other court, who would dally over chess with his ragged groom/squire. Close together like this, they looked a remarkable pair: the giant knight, neatly clad, combed to delight his lady; and the small, grubby groom whose smile showed no cringing servility. Like his mysterious background, like the occasional rages that blew away his reason, this unequal friendship was widely accepted as Sir Lancelot's eccentricity. Who would criticize Sir Lancelot and maybe have to face him?

Otter Mellias' dark face lightened at sight of me. He smiled up at me. Lugh scowled.

I said, "Lugh, I must talk with you." And sat down, uninvited, in the straw. It pricked through my flimsy gown and spread hay seed all over it.

Mellias set the chess board aside and made to rise. Lugh stopped him with a gesture. To me he growled, "Make it speedy." He did not want any connection with mages listed among his eccentricities.

We talked in whispers, for Lugh had nearly lost finger-talk.

"Brother," I said, "the crops are poor this fall."

Lugh shrugged.

"The farmers blame you. You and Gwen."

"Horse shit!"

"When the shortage is felt here in the dun your brother knights will blame you. Hostage Mordred will see to that."

Lugh spat. "It was your idea to bring him back here with us. I would have sliced his head off. Now he slithers about reminding folk of what they forgot before. I know what the adder wants. Do you know, Mage?"

Mellias signed to me, *Do not anger him!* I signed back, *This must be said.* But I drew back from Lugh. His giant hands were making fists. I whispered, "Mordred wants Caliburn and the crown, Lugh. What else?"

"The crown, God's balls! Mordred wants my rose!"

"Your rose?

Mellias signed, *The Queen.*

"You did not know that, wise Mage?"

Slowly, I admitted, "I was not looking in that direction." But looking there now, I thought of Mordred's dark, sidelong glances, and the way his teeth gleamed between slack, sensuous lips, and the way Gwenevere would walk far around, rather that brush against him.

Lugh muttered, "If he cannot have her he will destroy her." His fists opened and reached for a neck to wring. I drew farther away.

Mellias signaled, *All the time now he is close to rage. Do not press him.*

But I had to press him. I whispered, "Lugh. This thing, this rule you live by. Chivalry."

Lugh winced as though I had knife-pricked him.

"You remember, even as a boy you loved chivalry . . . you

thought it the highest way of life . . . Well, if I understand the thing rightly, chivalry means you love Arthur more than your life."

Lugh groaned. Sweat sprang out on his brow, spittle dewed his beard. Lugh hunched and rocked and moaned and sighed. At last he whispered, "Arthur can take care of himself. Know this." Another deep sigh. "I do love Arthur more than my life. But I love my rose more than Arthur. And . . . I do not know what to do! I do not know what to do! I do not know . . ."

I leaned to him and gazed into his anguished eyes. As an unborn child asleep in the womb wakes and stretches, so my sleeping power woke in me. I felt it stir, stretch and reach up my spine, between my shoulders, up the nape of my neck, through the top of my head. And I was inside Lugh's mind.

<hr />

Gwenevere sat at her loom, knees wide, freckled hands idle in her embroidered lap. A garden of stitched leaves and flowers crusted her overgown. I, Lancelot, drifted into her lap and the leaves and flowers came alive and aromatic. I smelled honeysuckle and rose. A skylark sang. A harp rippled sweet music.

I stood in sunshine with Gwen's arms tight around my waist and her cheek warm at my throat. I felt her soft heartbeat through overgown and tunic and breast. Folding her close, I folded the summer world to myself, this sweet earth and all her fruits and pungent herbs and fragrant flowers. Joy like sunlight flooded my world.

Now over the harp music I heard hooves strike rock. Saddles creaked, a horn winded. Knights rode by beyond the garden wall, red and white dragon banners flying. Arthur rode at their head.

I looked up.

Arthur turned in the saddle and looked straight at me—me, Lancelot—and I felt his gaze like a sword-thrust. A cry of grief escaped me.

My life was riding past. The Human glory I had sought, chivalry itself, was riding past. My King looked at me, and rode on. How gladly I would have given all that I had to ride with him! I would have sacrificed anything in the world . . . but my rose.

The knights passed. Hoof-beats and saddle-creaks faded in distance. Lark-song and harp music returned. But now came one solitary straggler, armed in black, riding a lean black charger. A raven's plume nodded from his black helmet. Under one arm he carried a golden grail. Opposite Gwen and me he drew rein and lifted this grail toward me, as though he asked a question.

I folded Gwen closer.

The black knight pressed heel to his thin horse and passed on. The horse's hooves raised no echo from the earth.

I, Niviene, had felt Lugh's despair. This was Human despair, for Human causes that should never have sullied my brother's mind. Now I searched through that mind for an edge of Fey forest, some lost memory or forgotten face I could seize and wield like a sword, to recall Lugh to his true self.

I found no Fey forest at all. No forest, no Lady, no Elana, no sister. In his own sight Lugh was truly Lancelot, wholly Human, a real knight bound by real chivalry to a real king.

Arthur appeared different to Lugh than to me. Where I saw a giant with a triple aura, heavy-fisted, high-minded and richly attractive, there Lugh saw his sworn king, his life's center.

I was astonished to see Gwen from Lugh's eyes. Here she seemed far lovelier, far sweeter, than I myself had found her; to me, Gwen was a beautiful Human woman like many another, small-minded, small-souled, wrapped in selfishness as in a cloak. To Lugh, she was the Goddess Herself, giver of life and joy, the world's heartbeat.

The world from Lugh's perspective appeared to me to be much as I would imagine it appears to most Humans. To most Humans . . .

Can you stop a swan from swimming?

Stealing a Human baby is almost as easy as stealing a loaf of bread.

Was my brother Lugh a changeling?

And hadn't I, in truth, suspected as much for years now?

Sad and shocked, I withdrew from his mind to find myself back in my body, all prickled in straw.

⌘

I had spent only a breath in Lugh's mind, but he had felt my entrance and withdrawal. He blinked, and drew a hand across his face.

I saw in Mellias' narrowed eyes that he knew what I had done.

So, now I knew Lugh's mind, what remained to be said? "Watch Mordred."

"Never fear for that!"

"And Aefa."

"Aefa? Your shadow?"

"She lies with Mordred."

"Like every slave girl in the dun."

For the sake of Arthur's Peace, I made one last weary effort. "Lugh. I have seen dread omens."

I went on to talk of dreams and ravens, owls, hawks and storms, some of them real omens Merlin had remarked, most invented on the spot. Lugh's big face darkened and paled and darkened again as I spoke; the Otter curled himself down small and rocked to and fro, either distressed or mocking me, I did not care which.

I finished: "Arthur's doom stands at his door, Lugh. Lancelot. Do not you be the one to open that door."

And I rose up, shook hay seed from my gown and left them there in the dim stable. I took myself off into sunlight.

10

MORDRED'S NIGHT

Under Counsel Oak's leafy roof I stand in twilight. Beyond his shade, autumn sun still filters through the apple trees of Avalon. I stand by the black cavern that lightning tore from Counsel's side long ago and look out at the golden light, and listen to Mellias trill his pipe, far away. I recognize the tune, a mournful little song called "Yellow Leaves." I am at home.

Out in the golden light five white deer search for fallen apples. One at a time they raise their heads—four smooth, one antlered—and look at me, and twitch uninterested ears. I am invisible. I am scentless.

A breeze stirs Counsel's leaves above me. "Har . . . vest" I think they say. I strain my ears but the leaves do not speak till flickered by the next breeze.

"Rest," they say, almost clearly. "Harvest, rest . . ."

Soon Counsel's leaves will fall. The God will die, to fill the Humans' barns . . .

"Fall," sigh the leaves. "You fall . . . we fall . . ."

A figure staggers out of shadow. Golden light strikes green on ragged gown, silver on long, wild hair.

The Lady reels among the white deer. No ear flicks, no head lifts. The Lady is invisible, scentless, like me. Her brown face has turned Anglo-white; under her rags she is spider-thin.

I yearn toward her. I step toward her, holding out supportive arms.

The Lady walks into my arms; into my chest; out my back; on toward Counsel Oak. I whirl. "Nimway!" I whisper. "Mother!"

She limps and lurches from sunlight into the shadow of Counsel Oak.

"Mama!"

With one skeletal hand she gathers her torn gown close.

"Fall . . ." the leaves murmur.

She bows her white head and steps into the black lightning-scar, into Counsel's side.

Far away, Mellias' pipe trills "Yellow Leaves."

Before my shocked eyes the lightning scar heals itself. Bark crawls across the entrance.

I run to Counsel Oak. I hammer my fists on his new bark. I tear at it with my nails. The cavern is sealed.

I start, a-tremble and awake.

Still deep in dream-dread, I lay frozen. Mellias' crystal burned against my throat. I opened my eyes and saw Merlin hunched like a shadow over our small fire. His long, even-lengthened fingers spun spells that flickered up the curving wicker wall. Mellias lay asleep on his pallet. Absent Aefa had not touched hers.

Something was amiss. I felt as though I had waked in the forest and sensed the approach of stealthy paws.

I felt as though an owl had called a name.

Beyond our wall the dun was tomb-quiet. Arthur and many of his knights were away. But a sentinel should have paced by on the hard-packed street. A baby could have cried in a nearby hut. Alley cats could have sung.

Merlin saw my open eyes and beckoned.

I struggled up, pulled on a shawl over my shift, and settled cross-legged at the fire, though I could not scry for Merlin. I wondered if he guessed that.

Merlin said with his fingers, *Aefa?*

I signed, *Mordred.*

Merlin grimaced. *Do not trust Aefa.*

Not now.

Aefa is man-crazy; Mordred is handsome.

I know.

We know what Mordred wants.

I thought of my journey into that dark mind and nodded. Merlin signed, *He will not wait forever.*

Arthur will not give him Caliburn!

No? Remember, Mordred is his nephew. Almost his friend. Mordred bade Arthur leave the dun tonight. Arthur left. Merlin leaned to me. *Niviene. Arthur's Peace nears its end.*

Yes.

Merlin had scried this in bird-flight, wind-shifts, stars, fire, water. I knew it as any Human might know it—by watching, listening, sniffing.

Merlin signed, *Mordred snakes. Mordred pokes here, there, under-foot, in pocket. Hisses of Gwenevere.*

I warned her she courts death.

Arthur will sacrifice her?

Yes, he will.

You know Arthur.

I stared into the flickering coals. Merlin sucked in his breath and uttered, "Hah!"

The sharp pain in my head was Merlin, withdrawing. As I fire-gazed, he had entered my mind. He stared at me, appalled. He signed, *Arthur's Peace is doomed because you lost power.*

I bowed my head.

Merlin thrust his hands under my nose to signal, *You love Arthur.*

I drew back away, insulted. *I cannot love.*

How often have you lain with Arthur?

Once. Twice.

Merlin assured me, *Your power will return. No one is always powerful.*

Even you?

Softly, he snorted. *Now you know Arthur. Will he sacrifice his wife, friends?*

Absolutely.

No doubt?

None.

When I led you here. The first day. Arthur knew you.

Yes.

You had met.

Yes.

Tell.

I translated one of Merlin's own songs into finger-talk. *Lonely hunter . . . enchanted wood . . . white deer . . . maiden.* And I added, *Flowering Moon.*

Merlin sat back to absorb this, his face in shadow. *Gods!* he signed, at last. *Good thing you let him live!* He thought further. I watched him make the connection he had to make. *Your child!*

I nodded.

Holy Goddess! Mother Earth! If I had known that . . . Merlin leaned back into light. The sorrow on his face nearly matched my own.

I knew his thoughts. My little Bran could have been Arthur's heir. Merlin could have carried him off to some monastery—maybe to Gildas—and had him taught. Merlin could have produced Bran as he had produced Arthur. Merlin could have been druid to three high kings—Uther, Arthur and Bran!

I shivered. My little Bran could have grown up Human. He could have joined battle and killed nine hundred men. He could have sat in judgment and ordered fellow Humans drowned or hanged. He might be alive today.

Or he might not. The Human world has its risks and dangers, and there is such a thing as Fate. But I was deeply glad that I had not known, myself, the identity of Bran's father.

The rustle of Mellias waking, rubbing his eyes and rolling over, startled this weird night's silence. Lithely he rose, pulled on his tunic and joined us at the fire. He whispered, "Our Aefa is still gone."

I said, "You know she is not 'our' Aefa, now."

To my horror, tears misted his eyes. He muttered, "This night is evil."

"You feel that, Mellias?"

"Even a Human would feel it."

Merlin whispered urgently, "Niviene! Look at the fire!"

"I cannot scry, Merlin."

"Pretend you can! Look, Girl, look."

Outside, a sound broke through the smothering curtain of silence. Muffled, padded feet stomped past our door—horses' hooves, clothed in rags.

Merlin whispered, "Niviene, scry!"

Mellias murmured, "Do neither of you mages hear horses?"

Bent over the fire, Merlin cried out, "Look here!"

As I bent over the fire, I felt Merlin's hand touch the base of my spine. From where his fingers lay, unlooked-for power wriggled up my back; and, even as I breathed a prayer of surprised thanksgiving, my eyes focused on the scene in the fire.

Naked and twined, Lugh and Gwen sprawled across a huge bed among rumpled linen sheets and embroidered cushions. A small oil lamp burned on a table. A red coverlet had been pushed to the floor. Love-making over, Lugh and Gwen petted and murmured. Lugh spread her hair in the lamplight and wound it around his arm. One of her pale hands fondled his chest. Their double aura had flamed red throughout the small room. Now it was shrinking and dimming to orange.

In the place where my heart had once lived, something hurt as though stabbed. Why did I have to be a "virgin" mage? At that moment I felt I would gladly be a mere Human queen, if I could live so in my body and treasure my heart!

Lugh lunged up on an elbow. Gwen pulled him down, but he struggled up again, head cocked, listening.

Gwen tensed, raised her head, and heard what he heard. She rolled over and reached down for the coverlet on the floor.

Lugh leapt up off the bed and looked wildly around him. The door—the heavy oak door, iron-bolted—buckled under blows from outside. Lugh rushed frantically around the walls, looking for a sword. The door splintered.

Lugh darted behind the door. On her feet by the bed, Gwen drew the red coverlet up around herself.

The iron bolt held, but the oak door broke vertically in half. Naked and empty-handed Lugh stood poised, concealed behind the open half-door.

A small dark man, sword in hand, rushed through the broken door and paused, his back to Lugh. Mordred. Over his shoulder I glimpsed other faces. For the space of a gasp Mordred stood, sword raised, peering around for Lugh.

I had thought of our hostage, Morgan's son, as a poisonous serpent who would lunge, then slither to cover. His courage surprised me. I would have expected to see him behind the men in the doorway, urging them on, not out in front. But there he stood like a rearing snake, eyes darting around the small, rich room.

Lugh struck. Clenched into one huge fist, his hands smashed down on the back of Mordred's neck. Mordred dropped. Lugh swooped, snatched Mordred's sword from his numbed hand and turned on the knights crowding in.

Those in front pushed back. No man would willingly fight Lancelot if he were armed. He stabbed a knight through the groin and whirled on another. Confused, the knights pushed back, knocked each other over and almost took flight.

Mordred reeled to his feet, pointing at Lugh. His mouth opened in a shout. The knights surged forward like a wave, attacking Lugh together.

Lugh backed across the room, slashing and parrying, leaving a man here, a man there, on the floor. He was making for a shadowed door at the back of the room which I thought led into Gwen's herb garden.

A small, cloaked figure slunk from the hall into the doorway. Aefa.

She bent and hefted a fallen sword and pushed it into Mordred's hand. Mouth wide in a triumphant cry, he followed the knights after Lugh.

All this time Gwen had stood statuesque, wrapped in her long hair and coverlet. Now she gathered up the coverlet, scurried to the herb garden door and shot back the bolt. Aefa glided from the doorway to plaster herself against a wall. Lugh pushed the garden door open with his shoulder and backed outside, parrying. Swords swinging, the knights pressed between him and Gwen. Lugh disappeared in the darkness outside. Mordred and two others seized Gwen by her hair, her arm, the coverlet.

The broken hall door glowed red. Arthur stood in the open half, armed, Caliburn himself in his gloved hand. His aura spread red through the room.

Our scrying fire flickered, flamed up once more and died.

A Merlin Song

This cauldron old and huge and dark,
Crusted with pictures rude and stark
Of stag and bull and captive bound,
Of naked God and druid gowned,
Once caught the blood of many a throat
While seers and sorcerers took note.
Now stands the druid, knife in hand.
Now all about the cauldron stand
King Vortigern, his Saxon Queen,
His knights and men-at-arms. The sheen
Of armor answers to the light
Of many a torch; around, deep night.
Out of the night the hunters come
Leading their prey. A single drum
Beats like a heart. Here stands the child
Whose father's unknown, of Hell or the Wild;
The child who was sought, and found, and brought,
The child whose blood in the cauldron caught
And mixed with mortar will save the fort.
He stands here before King Vortigern's court,
Looks calmly into King Vortigern's face,
And smiles with a quiet, friendly grace.
Breathes the Saxon Queen, "He shines like a star!"
Quick she moves, the knife to bar.
"Child," she says, "prophesy to the King.
Show him your word is a finer thing
Than your blood. Why does his fort not stand?"
Now, Merlin comes from a distant land.
He has heard no word of Vortigern's fort
That three times crumbled, as though the sport

Of angry God or teasing devil.
Calmly, he says, "Two dragons level
Your fort, my Lord, when they twist and fight.
They lie under the fort, one red, one white . . ."

11

GWENEVERE

Counsel Oak towers over all the ancient apple trees of Avalon. Oh, to rest once more in his shade, and hear once more his wise leaves whisper!

Here at Gildas' monastery, Arimathea, the apple trees were young, severely pruned, richly fruitful; like graceful maidens sporting red and yellow gems, compared to the hungry hags of Avalon, with their wizened brown treasures.

I crouched with Gildas in dappled shade, sorting apples. Ladders leaned and baskets waited throughout the orchard, young monks and village boys climbed and picked. (I was, of course, thought to be one of these boys.) Older monks trundled barrows from basket to basket and out to the apple sheds. Men called and shouted and sang here and there; barrows creaked, squeaked and bumped. Gildas and I talked softly, murmuring, whispering, hunched close together over our apple pile.

"Cider," Gildas muttered, and tossed the apple to his right. "Dry."

That apple plopped left. "So Niv, I ask you, what did you expect the King to do?"

A reasonable question. Why was I shocked? What would any Human king do, who saw his power threatened?

For fifteen years I had watched Arthur tolerate Gwen with something like affection, and sport with Lugh as with a brother. When the flash of his triple wide aura reminded me of his vast pride, I told myself, Never cross this man! I knew he could be dangerous to me; but Lugh was the man closest to him, and Gwen . . . he had lain with Gwen, and when she proved sterile he had not cast her off. There must be some tenderness there.

Gildas murmured, "You know he can't simply forgive his enemies like a Christian. No earthly king is so powerful he can do that."

A barrow squealed up to dump a fresh load of apples between us, then squeaked away.

My hands sank to my sides. The heart I did not have somehow clogged my throat and weighed me down, and something was happening to my eyes. Sun and shade ran together, and though my fingers touched apples I could not see them.

"Cry," Gildas advised. "Go right ahead and cry. Cider. Eat. Dry. You have shown remarkable courage, Niv, for a woman. Tomorrow you must be brave again, but you can take a private moment now to cry."

Tears blurred the light. My tears. And weird choking sounds erupted around the lump in my throat. I could not hold back either tears or chokes. Sobs.

Once begun, I could not stop. I muffled my sobs in my bunched tunic and crouched low behind Gildas. He shifted his bulk between me and most of the barrow traffic, but the orchard stretched all around us. I could only hope no monk would look down from his tree and notice that young Niv wept instead of working.

I cried hard for a while, letting anger and fear flow out with my tears. Then I cried now and then, and busied my hands in the apples between times. When at last I could speak—though still I could not see very well—I asked Gildas, "When did you know?"

"That you are a woman? I've known that since the day you watched me write, standing so close behind me. That day I smelled female. And I turned around and saw female."

"And . . . never said . . ."

"Do you say everything you know?" Gildas pulled a bit of cloth from his sleeve and handed it to me. "Clean up your face."

The dry, soft cloth comforted my face. "What is this?" I asked, wiping my hands dry too.

"It's a handkerchief, Mage. We civilized folk use handkerchiefs when we sneeze, or cry."

He had said "Mage." "You even know . . ."

"Every herd boy knows you for Mage Niviene, Merlin's assistant. We Humans are not stupid."

Now I could see Gildas smiling, wanting to hug himself for satisfaction, though his hands never slacked, tossing apples. He wiggled his brows at me and twinkled his eyes.

"Merlin said if you knew . . . or your brother monks knew . . . they would burn your books."

"I know you are not evil, Niv. Fifteen years you've been stopping here with Merlin, and no harm has come to monk, cow or corn. But as to burning my books, know you, Mage, I would sooner burn down Arimathea Monastery!"

I studied Gildas' merry, sympathetic face. When I had the power I had never read his mind; now it was closed to me. But I saw, looking carefully, how Gildas loved his books. When he said the word "book," his eyes brightened, and a tiny smile crept from the corners of his mouth. He held out a hand for the kerchief.

"I would like to wash this," I said, holding back.

Gildas grinned. "I do no magic, Niv. Your tears are safe in my hands." He reached and drew the kerchief from me. "I never thought to see these tears."

"I never thought to shed them!"

"Well, now we can be honest with each other."

"You know," I said, bending to the apples again, "it all began with you. All this came about because I told Arthur about your book."

147

"What!"

"Arthur was angry that you did not name him in your book."

Gildas made a sound between a growl and a hiccup.

"He does not know you are the author, Gildas. I would not tell him that. But he knows the book exists, and that he is not named therein."

Then I told Gildas how anger had turned to lust, how I lay with Arthur in the moonlit meadow and lost my power. "Mordred would never have trapped Lugh and Gwen if I had had my power. I never had even an inkling of what was to come. I left Merlin to work alone."

A barrow creaked nearby and Gildas bent quickly to his apple pile. "Eat. Cider." But he murmured exultantly, "The King knows! Now is my revenge perfect!"

I whispered, "Gildas. Is your revenge all that matters to you?"

Anger choked me like tears. Arthur was hunting Lugh like a wolf. The destruction of Arthur's Peace seemed imminent. And here heartless Gildas gloated over his worthless revenge! Who under heaven cared about what Gildas called "history"? Who even knew what it was?

I answered myself. Arthur knew, and cared.

Gildas chuckled. "Because you have given me revenge, Niv, now I will do what I can for you."

But I had never doubted that he would.

Riding the moonless night, hunting Lugh, I had told Mellias, "There is one who will help us. Abbot Gildas of Arimathea."

I heard the scowl in Mellias' voice. "A monk! A monastery! They will pull our filed teeth!"

"Gildas is Merlin's friend. I trust him."

"Hah! Well, if you come to grief, Niviene, I want to come with you." Mellias kicked his pony ahead.

His words sank into my mind and would have sunk into my heart if I had one. When I could trust my voice I called after him, "You're sure Lugh came this way?"

He flung over his shoulder, "If I ran naked I would make straight for our cave, like a wolf for his den."

I knew that Lugh and Mellias had a hideout somewhere in the low hills ahead. They had spent many a moon there, fishing and hunting, while the world thought Lugh sought the Holy Grail, or during one of Lugh's rages. They slept in a cave, caught and ate raw fish and sun-bathed by a stream. That was one reason Mellias stayed by Lugh. "I could never stay in the kingdom moons at a time," he said once, "if we did not come back to real life now and then."

Now we were making for this hidden cave. Shuddering, I imagined Lugh running, naked and barefoot, over this dark plain. He must have thrown himself flat when hooves thundered behind and thus escaped unseen.

We came to dark, crouching hills. We splashed across a stream. Mellias had no need to tell me how Lugh had crossed and recrossed this stream, how he had climbed this oak and swung through those beeches. I knew what I would have done, and where.

One thing Mellias could have told me, had I dared ask, was why he was guiding me on this hunt. I came after Lugh because I remembered being his sister, though he had forgotten me. Why did Mellias so endanger himself?

I dared not ask; but his crystal bounced warmly from breast to breast, reminding me of the almost Human warmth of Mellias' heart.

In a dark glade we slipped down and hobbled the winded ponies. Mellias led me by touch down a trail barely visible in moonless dark, even to us, across the stream once more, and up a cliff face. We crawled into the cave.

Now we couched in absolute darkness. "Lugh," Mellias murmured. And Lugh, back in the cave, whispered, "Mell!"

Mellias asked, "Do you have kindling?"

"In the fire pit."

Mellias said, "A good thing I brought fire!" He guided my hand forward to touch a pile of sticks and whispered, "You can still make fire."

"Still"? Did Mellias know about my night with the King? Now was not the time for questions.

I warmed my palms. Moments later a little flame, a little light, licked up. I looked around at the small, low cave, furnished with a few skins and pots. A grown Human could not stand up in here. Lugh could not stand up. Bone-lean, bloody and smudged, he lay curled against the back wall. He had rolled in mud to darken his skin. That was how he had gone unseen, flat on the breast of the Goddess, while his hunters galloped past.

His eyes closed against the light, then opened wide. "Niviene!"
Mellias chirped, "I brought her!"

Lugh unfolded, stood up stooping, came stooping to me. Wordless, he took me into his bare trembling arms. Mellias hugged us both, and the three of us nuzzled, chuckled and patted. In that embrace, I was almost glad of the danger and disaster that had brought us three back together.

Later, Lugh pulled on the clothes and wolfed down the bread that Mellias had brought. Wolfing, he asked, "Gwen?" Speechless, I looked at Mellias. Mellias looked away. Lugh gulped. "What has happened to Gwen?"

I tried to speak. Mellias' fingers rose and wriggled the basic sign, *Fire.* Lugh remembered that sign. The bread dropped from his suddenly slack hand into our fire.

Mellias signed again. *Unless you save her.*

༺∼ჟ∼༻

Arthur had ordered no hunt for Lugh's squire or sister, but (I told Gildas) Mellias and I took no chances. We lived in the dank, dim tunnel behind Merlin's hut and dug out an exit to the meadows. Merlin, of course, moved about freely. He was completely above suspicion. Had he not foretold the Queen's treachery long ago?

Aefa came to us there. Huddled by our brazier, shivering in the damp, we saw a lamp approach down the tunnel. A woman, richly gowned, carried the lamp before her. Standing over us she looked tall, till I rose slowly to face her. I said, "At least, you have not betrayed us."

"You knew I never would!"

"You betrayed Lugh."

"Lugh was nothing to me."

Ah. That was true. With close to Human folly I had supposed that if Aefa loved me, she loved my brother.

She said, "He will save Gwenevere." And she looked hard at us both. We looked back at her blankly.

She said, "It will be easy for him. To show respect, the knights about the stake will be unarmed."

Mellias sprang up. "Niviene, do not tell Lugh that!"

"Why not?" Groping through my confused knowledge of chivalry, I thought I knew why. But I could never be sure in these matters. Understanding chivalry was still like understanding Merlin's Latin stories, back in the villa. I did not really know the language.

Mellias sputtered, "Because if Lugh knew the knights were unarmed, he could not lift his sword! He would have to ride in there unarmed himself!"

Aefa said, "The stake is raised now, outside Queen's Hall." Merlin had told us that, too.

Mellias nodded. "We'll have to ride down three streets to the hall."

"Ride across," Aefa advised. "Between the huts." That made good sense. You do not stride down a forest path on a hunt, you slink through underbrush.

Aefa was saying, "Muffle the hooves. Lead the ponies. The whole dun will be looking at the stake, and if any do notice you . . . well, few would betray Sir Lancelot. Stop on the edge of the crowd and cut off the muffles." She hesitated. "I will cut them off for you."

I asked, "Aefa, are you hound or hare?"

"I hardly know, Niviene. Mordred . . . had me tranced. But you can trust me in this." I believed her. Actual tears stood in her eyes.

Merlin came scuttling down the tunnel. "Aefa, Mordred is calling for you. Hurry away." He seized her hand and pulled her back up the tunnel.

In the quiet dark, I asked the Otter, "Could Aefa have Human blood?"

"Not by the size of her!"

"She was crying."

"You don't need Human blood to cry."

Merlin scurried back to us, bent over his lamp like an ancient. He was showing his age. I thought of the Lady as I had dreamed her, white-haired and hesitant, and I shuddered. The elders walking ahead of me toward death were now so bowed I could see over their heads.

We could die with Lugh in this rescue attempt. I could die.

I said, "Merlin! Could we not simply leave here now and be gone?"

"Truly, you could." Merlin stroked his beard. "Are you willing to leave Lugh to his fate?"

I considered. Happily, with a sense of huge relief, I saw Mellias, Merlin and me riding away on a dark night, vanishing. Finding the odds hopeless, a Fey in his right mind would vanish.

Not so, a Human in love. I saw Lancelot charge through the crowd to the stake alone. I saw him pulled down, pressed under the weight of ten men. Caught. My brother, who once killed an adder for my good, who played with me on Apple Island, who guided me through the Children's Guard . . . caught.

"No," I realized aloud. "I cannot leave Lugh alone. Don't ask me why."

Mellias said, "Don't ask me why, but I can't leave Lugh, either."

"As for me," said Merlin, "I am half human. So I could never leave any of you."

I looked at the two faces close to mine in the lamp light, one white-bearded, wrinkled old man; one grinning, brown Fey. I held out a hand to each of them. Merlin sat down his lamp and took one hand, Mellias the other; and for a long moment we stood in silence, hand-fasted.

⸎

We led the blindfolded, muffled horses from hut to hut across the dun. We traveled each alone, one hut apart. Over thatched roofs and between huts growled the voice of the crowd about the stake in the center. "Fresh bannocks!" A hawker sang, and another, "Ale for sale!"

I shook my hooded head and muttered a curse on Humankind. A good thing it was for them that I had lost my power!

Lugh led the dapple-grey charger Mellias had stolen. Grey, said Mellias, would blend into the background better than the black of Lugh's own charger, and the great horse could easily carry two riders. For his strength, he lost something in speed, but we counted on the shock of surprise to delay pursuit. We had had to enlarge the entrance to our tunnel to lead the charger in, risking discovery with every spadeful.

Mellias and I led ponies, not so carefully chosen, that Merlin had sung in from the meadow. Well rested in the tunnel, they cocked their ears and danced sideways. Burdened by no baggage and bare-backed, once turned loose they would run like stags.

We all went cloaked, hooded and masked. Beside our knives, Mellias and I carried daggers, Lugh an ax and sword—not his own trusted sword that had won him fame and glory, but a stolen sword. Merlin had hefted it, laid his cheek to it, and declared it free of any powerfully evil aura.

Merlin was not with us. He had taken his "weapon," the harp Enchanter, elsewhere. I missed the sense of his steadying presence. Lugh's mind was bent entirely upon Gwen and the stake. Mellias thought first of Lugh. And I, leading my small brown pony forward toward the crowd, felt exposed and abandoned.

Hearing the crowd, my blindfolded pony bridled and balked. I blew in her nostrils, whispered in her ear, and pulled her along as a Human child might.

We came to the edge of the crowd. Over the milling heads—bare, hooded or veiled, none helmeted—I saw the tip of the up-thrust stake, surrounded by up-thrust lances—the lances we would have to pass, going in and coming out. At the back, knaves jostled and argued. But the knights in front stood silent, defenseless, heads bowed, as Aefa had told us they would. No one had told Lugh that.

I spared a bitter breath to imagine myself in Gwen's place.

A good thing I lacked the power to truly know! Imagination, common Human magic, has its own considerable power. Hastily, I backed myself out of that picture. Even a moment's imagination had drained needed energy.

Drawing my knife, I bent to cut the rags from the pony's hooves. Into my hood-narrowed vision came another knife, another small, brown hand. Aefa slashed the rags, straightened without looking at me, and disappeared.

I cut off the blindfold. The pony blinked and shied at the sudden light. Her small hooves danced eagerly. "A moment," I muttered in her ear. "A moment, and you can run your heart out."

I glanced right. A tall shadow-giant held a charger hard by the bridle.

A horn blew. The crowd shifted, sighed and fell silent to hear a herald announce Gwen's crime.

Till this moment I had moved as in a dream. I could not truly believe that Arthur would order this, or that his knights would stand and witness it, or that Humans of all stations would stand and gawk at it, hoisting their children on their shoulders to see it.

Now came the fire, real, alive, and I had to believe what I saw.

Reaching the stake, the torches dipped down out of sight. A whiff of smudged smoke rose over the watching heads. The crowd gasped and shuddered and craned its neck.

I grasped the little mare's mane and swung onto her back.

To my right, the shadowy figure crossed itself with the Christian sign and mounted the shadow horse.

I kicked the mare into action.

She trotted into the crowd, knocking knaves, slaves and hawkers aside. She did not want to trample people, but I kicked her fiercely forward. The smell of smoke frightened her, the tension all around, and now the sound of crackling flames. Now squires and men-at-arms went down under hoof, cursing and flailing, and we were in the front row among the bare-headed knights.

Tight faces turned to us. Some of them I knew: Gawaine, Geheris, Bedevere. I drew my dagger, and the unarmed giants retreated quickly, in good order, leaving a clear path to the stake. None raised hand or voice. Later, Lugh would remember this to his unbearable sorrow.

Between me and the stake, faggots were beginning to burn. The flames still crackled low, but would leap at a breath. Gwen leaned against the wooden stake. Smoke already stained her white shift; flames licked at her feet.

Lugh checked the charger beside me. Ax in hand, he leapt straight onto the pyre. The charger wheeled away, but I caught his rein.

As when I once held two coracles together in mid-flood, one in each hand, so now I held two panicked animals together. The charger snorted and sidled, the little mare shrieked. Both backed into the crowd. Behind me I heard groans, orders, running feet. Because of my mask I could see nothing to the side; I only saw Lugh, straight ahead, chopping the stake down.

Flame flared between us. The stake toppled. Lugh leapt through the flame, Gwen like a white sack on his shoulder. (Had the fool woman fainted?)

Lugh slung her onto the charger and vaulted up behind. She came to enough to grab the horse's mane and add her bare-heeled kicks to Lugh's. He seized the rein from me, wheeled the charger and gave him his head.

A swinging section of stake still chained to Gwen hit my mare a vicious blow on the haunch. She reared and shrieked again, and I caught her mane to hold on.

A small brown hand seized my rein and hauled us after Lugh. Mellias and I thundered after the dapple-grey rump fast disappearing behind a cloud of smoke and dust. The piece of stake swung, beating the charger to his best speed.

Aefa had told us rightly; the whole dun—knaves, men-at-arms, knights, nobles—was gathered about the stake. Galloping down narrow streets to South Gate we met not a soul. Behind us, the voice of the crowd roared, then sank into distance. Tunnel-visioned, Mellias' hand firm on my rein, I pounded along in Lugh's dust as though kidnapped.

South Gate loomed before us, a narrow gap in the rampart. The iron gate stood wide on its iron hinges and beyond, glimpsed through dust clouds, the meadows stretched to safety.

Like story-enrapt children three burly guards hunkered down left of the gate. A white-bearded bard sat on a stone before them, even-lengthed fingers on his harp strings. Beside him, a small black pony hung her unkempt head.

We thundered down upon them. White-beard played on with never a glance our way. The grey charger pounded through the gate.

Up leapt the guards, swords screeching from scabbards.

Up leapt Merlin, harp in hand, and vaulted astride the black pony. From a dejected standstill the pony flew into a gallop, hurtling through the gate just ahead of Mellias and me. A javelin whizzed past Mellias' nose and thudded into Merlin's side. Merlin fell forward on the pony's neck and hung on.

We were through and out and streaking across the meadows.

I tore off hood and mask. Sudden light flooded my eyes, meadows bounded past. A flock of sheep drew away from us with shuddering cries. Grazing oxen raised arching horns to stare at us. I listened for hoofbeats behind and heard none.

Aefa had turned every horse in the dun loose on the meadows.

156

Gildas' eyes were dark with concentration. He stared at me, brows twitching and rumpling. Spilling the story, I had tossed apples hither and yon as though sorting, without looking at them. Gildas had given up the pretense and listened with folded hands.

When my voice died away in a weepy quaver, Gildas said quietly, "And you made your way here by an unknown way."

"Merlin knew the way. But Arthur must be close behind us. With Merlin hurt, we traveled slowly."

"Our healers are skillful, but . . . you know he has a bad wound there."

"Yes."

"Look, Mage Niv. Arthur will respect our right of Sanctuary for a time. But the Queen's presence here is a . . . desecration."

I turned a bitter laugh into a hiccup.

"She is an unacceptable burden to us. This night she must go on to St. Anyes, disguised as a monk."

"St. Anyes?"

"A convent, half a day's ride. I thought you knew all this country."

"Not all. Only from our forest to Arthur's dun, and north to Morgan's Hill."

Gildas' brows shuddered. "Play with serpents, they bite."

"So they did, Gildas."

"The King will respect Sanctuary, I would not guess how long. In the end, horse and ax are stronger than pious words."

"Arthur is truly pious."

Arthur was two men, as his auras proclaimed. There was the red and orange king, who for his pride would hunt his friend and burn his wife; and there was the great golden soul, devoted to his country and his people, sacrificial beyond the scope of most Humans, and to us Fey perfectly incredible. And that Arthur was as real as the bloody-handed chief who yet hunted us. I murmured, "When Arthur comes, convince him to turn monk. He could work miracles, Gildas. He could be your church's greatest saint in history." Gildas chuckled. "I do not joke." Gildas laughed.

A barrow creaked nearby. Gildas called, "We have mixed the piles here. Give us time." He bent to re-sort my wildly flung apples. Past our shade, in the mellow sunlight, the monk blinked and paused. Then he trundled his barrow away.

I, too, sorted apples, this time more carefully. I murmured, "So Arthur comes and besieges Arimathea, and you hold him off for a time with the right of Sanctuary. Then what?"

"Then he comes in, swinging his magic sword, and finds you flown."

"You will send us all away, like Gwenevere?"

"This very night. The Queen goes to St. Anyes. You and Sir Lancelot and his groom and my old friend go on to your enchanted forest."

"But Gildas . . . Merlin can barely ride."

"Merlin will have to ride, or face Arthur as a sacrificial lamb."

It would not be the first time Merlin had been cast in that role. His magic had saved him as a child before King Vortigern, as prophecy poured from his lips. This time, old and sorely wounded, he might not be able to summon up power.

I said slowly, "Gildas, I fear he will die on the way."

"Then that will be his fate. But surely, Mage, you are a healer? You can save him."

"I know not." Even when my power was at its height, healing had not been my best gift.

Gildas laid a gentle hand on my shoulder.

Thinking him heartless as myself, I had mistaken Gildas. Now I felt his heart through his hand. Very Human it was, warm and steadfast to the point of folly.

He snatched it away. He had forgotten my sex. Most likely, Gildas had not touched a female shoulder since he hugged his mother goodbye and set off for Arimathea, forty years gone. He said firmly, "Take your friends to your forest, whether that be in this world or another. And come here no more, Mage Niv."

We rode a day out from Arimathea across rolling meadow lands and fields full of harvesters. Some of these still sweated in standing grain; others celebrated Harvest Home with dance, song and play sacrifice. We passed laughing men binding a pretty girl in stalks. Lugh turned around on his charger to tell me, "Now they will throw her in the river." I was not much surprised. These were Humans, after all. "See," he said, "the bindings are loose. And the river is shallow."

He led us on his great grey charger. Without armor he was no great weight for the horse, who stepped out proudly, glad of the exercise. We had chosen this horse for endurance and "invisibility," and now he showed another benefit: respectability. Peasants who saw him approach moved quickly aside, though his rider wore rags. The charger would pace grandly by them, followed by a hurt old man and two dwarves, or children, on ponies. I wondered what stories the peasants told of us in their taverns.

Lugh rode easily, quiet and alert. I knew that since he had kissed his rose goodbye (while we looked carefully away), his thoughts had ridden with her. Every hoofbeat bore him farther from her. But once, when passing clouds misted the autumn sun, I saw his aura stream away behind him, a thread of gleaming energy spinning out like a spider's web to Gwen.

(I saw it! "Gods," I murmured to myself. "I can see!" And then I saw nothing because grateful tears blinded me.)

Lugh's loneliness for Gwen was burden enough for a fragile mind that had cracked a few times before now. Added to this, his remorse for his friends almost overbore him. Once safe, with a good head start, Lugh remembered that his brother knights around the stake had been unarmed. "I struck them down," he told me, numb with grief. "I don't remember which. I remember faces looking up at me, but not which faces. And I struck. Oh, holy God!"

I thought, *In the forest, he will heal. He will come back to his true*

159

self . . . if it was his true self . . . He will come back to the Lugh he
used to be, the big, blunt, straightforward brother I remember.

I was glad that Lugh led us. His responsibility for us held him
together under grief and remorse and self-horror.

Behind Lugh, Mellias led Merlin's pony on a trace. Merlin
slumped sideways. We stopped where we found occasional shelter
to dress his wound, which kept breaking out and bleeding afresh.
And in the shade I saw that his aura had shrunk from an extensive
white mist to a narrow orange flicker.

As the sun bent toward the western hills Lugh waved an arm and
pointed, and we saw on the horizon a low, dark smudge, a forest.
This forest was not ours. We had taken a new track, swinging wide
of the area Arthur would search. But forest it was, dark, sheltered,
homelike. Even bent, gasping Merlin smiled.

Closer, we paused to deck ourselves and Lugh's charger with
identifying herbs. Small, dark children might wait for us in the
trees, gleefully counting their poisoned darts.

We entered at sunset. The horses bridled and snorted as the forest dark reached out to them, laden with wild smells.

Merlin lay flat along his pony's back and buried his face in its
mane. His wound had opened and was dripping a faint blood-trail.
We three slid down and led our mounts along the narrow trail,
between snatching brambles and under arching branches. Lugh
went first, then Merlin, then myself, and Mellias last.

I watched the highest treetops, still sunbright above us. Birds
and squirrels flew and chattered, but I was sure no invisible cloak
swirled, no glinting dark eyes followed our progress with hostile
curiosity, no fingers itched to let fly a dart.

Mellias said softly, "Fey are gone from this forest. Only wolves
will greet us."

No one questioned him. Lugh was searching the trail. I was re-
laxing, breathing moss, bracken, fern, serpent, toad, Goddess in
the air.

Twenty years gone, returning to Avalon after the Children's
Guard, I had felt like this. Coming home to our forest from Arthur's

kingdom I had always felt like this, as though I woke from a troubled dream and found my mother's arm thrown lightly over me in
the safe warmth of our bed-robe.

Yew and oak and ash embraced each other over the vanishing
trail. Small creatures fled through bracken. The Goddess leaned
from the darkening sky and breathed upon us. The uneven trail led
across Her knees. Her spread hands received us.

Surely the Goddess was my enemy. For fifteen years I had not
sacrificed to Her. My one child was dead, and my fruitful years
were passing. The day would come when I could no longer accept
Her gift of life and give life back to Her. Surely She hated me.

But I walked gladly into Her hands. I rejoiced as I felt Her breath
on my face. Does a mother hate her rebellious child? And what
little one, tantrum over, does not return trustfully to its mother's
arms? Like such a little one, I returned to the breast of the Goddess.

Out in the kingdom the sun was now set. Our trail darkened till
our Fey eyes widened; Human Lugh could most likely not see at
all.

"Lugh," I said, "we should stop. Merlin—"

Merlin heaved himself upright and urged his pony past the
charger. "Here," he croaked, pointing. "We go in there." And he
rode straight into the dark between two towering beeches.

Lugh stood amazed. He had led us to this point; now sick old
Merlin suddenly seized command and left him blind in the dark.

"Catch him," Mellias advised in a voice touched by laughter. I
turned to him, happily surprised. I had not heard that note in his
voice for days. Mellias, like me, revived in the forest. His small dim
figure had straightened, his eyes glinted.

Lugh mumbled a curse, dismounted and led the charger after
Merlin. The great horse could not easily step through underbrush,
and moved slowly. We followed his pale rump through thick young
trees. "Lugh," I ventured, "I could go first." With my Fey night-
vision.

The charger stopped and blew. Past him, I saw a small red
flicker—a fire in a stone circle. Cautiously, Lugh pulled the horse

forward. We followed them into a dim-lit clearing where Merlin stood, bent over, clasping his side.

In the midst reared a giant oak fringed with mistletoe. A rickety ladder led up to a wicker tree-house that reminded me of Aefa's old den. A rich scent of cooking nut mast filled the clearing and waked hunger. Chestnuts, beechnuts and hickory nuts roasted in an iron pan on the fire-stone. I licked my lips and swallowed. We had last eaten at Arimathea.

Another scent lingered under the scent of food. The clearing smelled of . . . Human. A Human lived here alone. But the solitary life is contrary to Human nature. Humans live in packs.

Ghosts drifted here, too. My tingling skin signaled their presence—ghosts, and higher spirits, such as those that haunted the Arimathea chapel.

I saw that Merlin did not dare raise his voice. The effort might open his wound. I whispered, "Lugh, call out. Announce us." For Lugh was staring about like a child who waits to be led.

At my bidding, he called, "Hola, ho!" in Angle and "Hail, Friend," in Latin.

"Hola," a gentle voice answered from above in rough, peasant Angle. "Merlin, old friend, is that you I see?" From the tree-house leaned a dim face.

Merlin raised his voice enough to say, "Caleb, it is I, with friends."

"I must have known a crowd was coming, I cooked all my mast! But you are hurt . . ." For Merlin had folded to the ground.

Mellias and Lugh settled Merlin leaning against the oak. Caleb climbed down, squirrel-quick. He was tall, but too thin and gentle to call a giant. Close to, he smelled sour. Between his rough brown hair and beard his face was ageless, unlined, utterly free of all traces of Human fantasy, greed or grief. Such a face might belong to a Fey, or an idiot. But wisdom looked out of Caleb's eyes.

"Let me tend that wound."

From a storage hut back in the trees he brought herbs I did not know, and some kind of berry-oil. From a nearby spring he brought clear water. While he dressed the wound he never glanced at the rest of us. He trusted us, for Merlin had named us friends.

Mellias hobbled the horses. Lugh squatted by the fire and drooled at the roasting mast.

Merlin's wound staunched and bandaged, Caleb sat back on his heels. And now he looked us over with quiet eyes.

Merlin murmured, "Caleb is a Christian hermit."

That much I had guessed. He reminded me of some of Gildas' brother monks, those with great white auras. In the dark I could not see his own.

Merlin nodded toward Lugh. "Sir Lancelot is one of the King's knights."

Anywhere in the kingdom, those words would have raised ex-cited hands and voices. I felt that Caleb had heard the name before, but seeing the man did not break his shell of calm. He looked past Lugh to Mellias and me.

"Mellias," Merlin wheezed, "and . . . Niv . . . are of the Fey."

Mellias and I bristled and crouched like hunting dogs, ready to spring. Never, in fifteen years, had Merlin announced this fact aloud. Humans fear and hate the Fey, and Christians connect them with their evil God Satan.

Caleb sat on his heels, unmoved.

And Merlin gasped, "Niv is a woman." So he took and tossed away our last armor of deceit.

Caleb smiled at me and said, "A beautiful woman," like a court-ier.

His smile brightened the firelight. I took a deep breath and felt his aura brush peacefully against mine. I knew then that it was enormous. That aura could fill this clearing and expand into the forest, or seek out a spider in its web, if Caleb wished it.

Mellias slumped down beside me. Caleb turned his smile to him and said, "The mast is cooked."

We ate close around the little fire while the horses snuffled hun-grily in the dark. "Keep them close," Caleb warned, "or wolves may get them."

Otter Mellias said, "Wolves may get them here, Caleb."

The hermit shook his head, no.

We ate the mast, not out of the pan, but from a treasure—a large, round dish that, in the firelight, glinted like silver. In truth, it was silver, tarnished and dented, but true. Now how had a greed-free hermit come by this grail?

Round our circle it went, emptier at each passage. Caleb did not eat. He would hold the mast under his nose a moment, breathe in the mast aroma, then pass it on to Mellias. I wondered if he lived often on the smell of food. I had heard such tales of Christian saints, and Caleb was thin enough.

The empty, finger-scraped dish ended in Merlin's hands. He lay down, rested his head on Mellias' knee and turned the grail round and round in his gaunt hands, learning it.

At last he said, "This . . . rich treasure."

I was embarrassed for him. I had never seen him so Human before—fussing like a housewife over a dish. "Where did you find this, Caleb?"

"It was my mother's."

"I'll wager it was her mother's, too."

"You win your wager."

"Ah. And that is why . . . you keep it by you . . . this share of greed and sin?"

"I see no greed in it, Merlin. No sin." Caleb reached for his grail, but Merlin hugged it.

"Men would do murder for this dish," he chuckled, and stiffened in pain.

Caleb warned, "You are talking too much."

Merlin struggled to sit up, but lay on his elbow instead, staring down into the grail under his nose. He cleared his throat, spat to the side, and announced, "This silver dish of your mothers is in truth the Holy Grail, for which knights seek and monks pray. You did not know this?"

Caleb's eyes widened.

I had not believed the Grail existed. I sat up straighter, eyes fixed upon it.

Merlin tried to sing. He quavered, *"The Holy Grail we see, angel-revealed to me, Tarnished though it may be, Christ's cup verily . . .* Oh, Gods!" He spat blood.

Caleb said only, "Merlin, do not sing. Do not talk."

Merlin set the Grail down close to his side, raised his hands and signaled, *You knew this!*

We watched, dumbfounded. I had never before seen a Human follow finger-talk. I had somehow assumed that they could not, that they were debarred from learning.

Caleb answered aloud. "No. I knew only that it came from my family."

You never felt power flow from it?

"Only the power of love."

"If I could sing! I would sing of the folk who wait for the Grail to shine on them. Knights. Merchants. Peasants. Romans. And here you eat nuts from it! Any church or monastery in the world would give all they possessed to keep this Grail for the healing of the world!"

And Caleb said, "Merlin. Take the Grail. Bestow it where you will, for the healing of the world."

Merlin beamed embarrassing, greedy joy. Then he sobered. "Friend," he said softly, "I know your sacrificial heart. Can you . . . live without the grail of your mothers?"

Caleb shrugged. "If I cannot live without this thing, or any other thing, I might as well go back to the civilized world with you." Merlin nodded and stroked the Grail as he might stroke a cat. "But you cannot leave here soon, Merlin."

"In the morning."

Caleb shook his head. "That wound . . ."

Merlin spoke to Caleb with his fingers.

Very quietly, I reached and took the Grail. I fingered it, caressed it, rubbed till it shone; with the shine came faint impressions, through my fingers, or through other senses. Had I my full power they would have been much stronger. But I was pleased to find any impressions. Maybe, I thought, my power was creeping back to me . . . or maybe the Grail's power augmented mine.

I felt the warmth that Caleb claimed to feel; a warmth of love, that same presence I used to feel in Human huts which, as a child, I entered to rob. I heard soft voices, as of a family beside a hearth; I smelled oats, bran, peas. At one moment the Grail weighed in my hands as though laden with a feast; the next moment it practically floated away, light as an empty stomach. I saw a mother spread a few peas in the dish to look like many. I saw her watch the children eat. Silently I asked the Grail, *How were you made?*

Long, long ago in Roman days the Grail was fashioned by a coarse-muscled giant who sang at his task and sold the piece for bread. He had no thought of power beyond the power of making.

I heard Caleb say, "If only you could sing for us!"

Faintly, Merlin whispered, "I could try . . . Enchanter is yonder, on the pony."

"Do not joke, Merlin." And Caleb said to Mellias and Lugh, "You know, Merlin can sing tales of the saints, as well as tales of knightly combat."

Merlin chuckled and boasted, "A real bard can sing any tale, any-where. Any language."

No spiritual power dwelt in the Grail, nor ever had.

Merlin was lying.

❧

Wolves came in the night.

Caleb had warned us. "Give them no power," he said. "Pay them no heed." (Just as the Lady had once said of my ghosts, "Give them no power." But these were material wolves.)

The ponies did not understand this. Their whickers and whinnies woke us to the sight of lean, dark shapes circling the clearing.

Caleb had told us that most nights he slept up in the tree-house.

But the house could not hold us all, nor could Merlin climb the ladder; so in courtesy Caleb lay with us close to the fire, and shared his flea-hopping blankets with us. Now he sat up and spoke firmly to the wolves. "Shoo," he told them, as a peasant might tell his dogs, "Out. Go. These folk are my guests, and the horses too. Leave them alone."

Then Caleb lay back down, rolled over and snored.

By all Gods! How had this fool ever attained his present age?

I sat up, gathered what power I could, and produced my silver, sparkling light-shield. I tried to spread it around the whole clearing, but it spread thinly.

The wolves paused to look up at it, and gnash and slobber among themselves. Very like dogs they looked in the low firelight; I knew they were less dangerous than dogs, but I was not going to lie down and snore in their presence!

As one wolf, most of them suddenly turned tail and left the clearing. A few sat down on the edge and drooled at us.

I lay awake, tossing between snorting Caleb and moaning Merlin. Twice in the night I rose to renew my shield as it faded. The first time I noticed the wolves had lain down, tongues lolling. They watched almost indifferently as my white mist rolled and spread through the clearing. The second time, they were gone.

Power aroused, I could not now lie down and sleep. I sighed, and looked around in the dimming dark. Morning waited a little eastward. Our fire was out.

Otter Mellias said, "Use your power to light the fire. I'll get sticks."

I turned to him, where he lay rolled up in a tattered robe of Caleb's. "How do you know I have power to use?"

He smiled at me. "Niviene, what do I not know about you?"

While I pondered this he rose and went out among trees we could now see quite well. He made not the slightest sound as he gathered a stick here, a fallen branch there, and came like a shadow back to my elbow. He crouched and piled the wood in the stone circle. I crouched beside him and laid my palms to it and whispered, "What do you know about my high power, Mellias?"

He signed, *Dead as this fire.*
"And why is this so?"
The King.
By the Gods, he did know!
Mellias, by what power do you know all this?
"That you know, Niviene."
"I do not!"
Mellias grinned at me as the fire flared alive.

⚜

Lugh said, "I stay here."

I stared at Lugh. My stomach (so soon empty again!) dropped into my boy's boots. After all these years of human life! After forgetting his home and heritage for so long! Now, as at last we neared our Forest, Lugh would abandon us again.

He turned to Caleb. As an afterthought he asked him, "You will take me as an apprentice hermit, will you not?"

We stood ready to leave, Merlin already bowed in pain to his pony's neck. He grunted strong disapproval. I saw my own desolation mirrored in Mellias' brown eyes. He looked hopefully to Caleb; and to my relief and joy, I saw that Caleb struggled with himself. His great white aura shivered.

I thought, Hah! Caleb waits happily for us to depart and leave him in peace with his wolves and his God! He will reject Lugh. Surely, he will reject Lugh.

But Christian Charity—that strange, nonsensical virtue—forbade outright rejection. Here was a soul in need. Only a soul very much in need would wish to stay in this haunted clearing.

Lugh noticed Caleb's struggle. Surprised, he sought to explain himself. "I would be a hermit like you, Caleb. I would live in peace with God's creatures and contemplate God for the rest of my life. Accept me as your apprentice, or your disciple."

Caleb gave a slow shrug and the dull cloud spread all over him like a cloak. Slowly, he said, "Friend Lancelot, I have heard of you."

"Even here!" Lugh's mouth tweeked in a brief smile.

"I have heard of your sudden rages. You can rush away in a rage and be gone for a season, no man knows where. You can kill without intention. You are a fine fighting man. I do not think you would be a good hermit. You have not that gift."

Lugh spread begging hands. "Caleb, you can heal me of these rages! You can teach me peace!"

From his pony, Merlin groaned impatiently.

Caleb muttered, "I eat no meat. I do no harm."

"I, too, will do no harm."

"I pray from noon till dark."

"I will not disturb you."

"Why? Why would you give up the world and stay with me?"

And Lugh said, "I have lost the world. I have lost King, and honor, and love. I may as well turn to God."

Caleb laughed. The dull cloud rolled a little away as laughter swayed his thin form. He said with relief, "You will not remain here long."

"I will!" Lugh insisted. (He did not realize how little Caleb wanted his company! He would have done better to agree that his stay would be short; but Lugh was never perceptive.) "I will stay here forever and eat nuts and mushrooms and preach to the birds!" A small excitement brightened his face as hermiting took on an adventurous hue. "And you will heal me, Caleb! I shall know peace!"

Caleb looked around for help, to sky, earth and the silent trees. He was inspired. "This life is not all prayer. Will you gather wood and scavenge food?"

Lugh swallowed. This thought of work and scavenging came hard to Arthur's best knight. But he said, "I will."

Caleb looked up to the brightening tree tops. "Lord," he prayed aloud, "grant us a sign. If this unhappy friend should stay with me, grant us a sign."

His voice echoed from the close trees and died away. I waited to see what magic Caleb could call up; and almost instantly, the bracken behind me rustled and snapped. I whirled. The horses shifted and blew.

Through the underbrush pushed a great white creature, crowned with branches. Regal as Arthur, a white stag stepped quietly into Caleb's clearing.

Caleb laughed for joy. "Cervus!" he called, as to a welcome friend. "Cervus, show us the Lord's will!"

The stag scanned us all with calm, dark eyes. Against the undergrowth he shone like a snow statue, and his star-sparkled, orange aura twinkled wide around him; animal spirit mingled with higher spirit. He dipped his antlers and came toward us.

The horses drew back uneasily at his approach. Slowly he passed between Mellias and me, pausing to point his antlers inquiringly at each of us. Close to, he smelled like any autumn stag, of grassy sweat and semen. But as he paced toward Caleb the natural orange faded from his aura, leaving only a starry foam. Cervus moved now in a dream, forgetting his true nature, governed by spirit.

Caleb asked more softly, "Cervus, shall this man remain with us?" And he pointed at Lugh.

Head low, mighty antlers swinging, Cervus approached Lugh.

Lugh clapped hand to knife.

Good! I thought, *Good! Let Lugh stab Cervus, and come away with us!*

Now Cervus stood before Lugh, head turned slightly to look him eye to eye. Lugh stepped back. Slowly, he lifted hand from knife. Slowly, Cervus stepped forward and rested his heavy head on Lugh's shoulder.

Resigned, Caleb came and embraced man and stag. "It is the Lord's will," he declared sadly, rubbing Cervus' neck like that of a horse. "You shall stay with us, Lancelot. May God heal you of your rages."

12

COUNSEL OAK

On a shaded stone table between wood and pasture we found three small loaves of bread, one of them warm. I slid down from the grey charger Lugh no longer needed and seized the loaves. They had been left here for the poor, the homeless or the Good Folk. We were all three.

Mellias helped Merlin down from the charger where I had held him before me. We settled down by the stone and dressed his wound while the hobbled horses grazed.

When we lifted Caleb's bandage, the wound sickened us. It reeked. The wound itself had turned black and crackly. Around it, Merlin's side oozed pus. We needed more than Fey determination to stay here beside it; to not sneak quickly away, grab the ponies and disappear.

Mellias looked at me over Merlin's lolling head. Our eyes met and we nodded.

Caleb had known. His last words to me were, "My old friend longs to reach a certain tree, one Counsel Oak. You know this tree?"

"I know it well."

"Do not spare him on the journey. Ride there, direct and swift."

"But his wound . . ."

"Will not matter."

So I knew in what case Merlin stood. I had the word of a healer more skilled than myself.

Otter Mellias went off to seek water. Merlin sat leaning against the stone table, panting and twitching. Beside him, I sat on my heels, looking out over pasture land to the smoke of a hidden village. Sheep drifted far out; their calls trembled the air. On the edge of hearing, a shepherd's pipe sang.

Close by, the hobbled charger limped after grass. In his saddle-bag, Enchanter and the Holy Grail clanged gently.

"Merlin," I said, "you said the Holy Grail would heal the world. Can it not heal you?"

Painfully, Merlin chuckled. "Oh Niviene! Grown up long ago and still an innocent!"

I bit back an angry retort. Merlin sighed and went on, feebly. "I invented the Holy Grail to discredit the Christians. I thought . . . when no Holy Grail ever appeared . . . shining . . . magically engraved . . . they might think again about their religion. But now I see . . . that was my worst mistake. For I have made mistakes, Niviene."

I said, to comfort him, "You are half Human, after all."

"Niv, I charmed Lugh and Gwenevere to love each other."

I sat stunned. I could think of no response. Finally, I stammered, "Whatever for?"

"I thought Arthur would cast her off. Her stars were wrong. She was wrong for his Peace . . . but Arthur closed his eyes. Like King Mark."

"Yes."

"And now my mistake has cost him his crown."

"Arthur still wears his crown."

Merlin rolled his head against the stone: No. "At this moment he rides to battle against nephew Mordred for the crown."

"So that's why we've seen no sign of him!"

"He has more than us to worry him." Merlin closed his eyes and seemed to nap uneasily, twitching and starting and rolling his head. The distant sheep drifted closer, and the voices of shepherd children mingled with their bleats.

Eyes closed, Merlin said, "Niv, go to the battle for me. Do for Arthur what I would do."

"Where?"

"I'll tell you all . . . later." I wondered if later he would be able to speak, or even sign. He sighed deeply. "Mordred was also my mistake. I brought him back from Morgan's Hill."

"Yes. Don't talk any more. Just rest."

He shook his head, grimaced. "And . . . about Mordred . . . Niv, you must forgive me."

I turned my eyes from the sheep and the distance to stare at Merlin. Never does Fey say to Fey, "Forgive." This is a purely Human concept. Slow with wonder, I asked, "I? Forgive you? For what?"

"You will learn. When you learn . . . forgive."

As the flock came closer, the herd children saw us. They wielded furious staves and whistled their dogs to turn the sheep aside. We were strangers, perhaps desperate folk—maybe even the fearful Fey, for whom bread was left on the stone table.

Merlin gasped, "The Holy Grail was my worst mistake of all. I invented it to . . . confound the Christians. But it confirmed them."

"How is that, Merlin?"

"Had it been found. Had a grail been found and named and placed on an altar. Then even Humans would see that it was only a thing. Just a material object."

"Not if it worked miracles." Human faith can work its own miracles. Hand a dying Human a handful of hair, tell him it came from the head of Joseph of Arimathea, and he may well recover.

Teeth clenched, Merlin hitched himself higher up against the table. He turned misted eyes toward the bleating flock, but I did not think he could see much. "It would remain a thing . . . and one day, finally, they would see that, and cease to worship it . . . and what it stood for. But . . . the Grail will never be found. I will not be here to find it."

"It's over there in your saddlebag."

"They would never accept that one, Niv. Not that dented, worn dish."

"Then why did you take it from Caleb?"

"I did not take it from Caleb! I persuaded him to give it for the healing of the world."

"But why? Why?"

"Because that Grail is holy. Did you not feel its power?"

"Merlin, I knew you were lying when I felt no power in it. I felt only . . . love. Human love."

"Yes. The holiest power in the world. That Grail will heal your life, and perhaps Arthur's life. And that healing will spread."

The Grail would heal my life? I hardly knew that my life was wounded. I listened, entranced, to Merlin's stumbling, halting words.

"In time, Niv . . . in the course of time, flowing like water . . . like the Fey river . . . all life flows together. Like streams into the river. The time will come . . . when Angle, Saxon, Roman will mean nothing. Even Fey and Human will mean nothing . . . They will all flow together . . . and divide into yet new streams . . . and those will flow together . . . like water, Niv. Life is like water."

And as Merlin paused, panting, I seemed to see the Fey river as though I floated above it. I saw streams join it here and there, and lose themselves in its flood. I saw streams flow from it, branch away and join it again.

Merlin said, "Life is one, Niv. Separation is only for a while. So when the Grail blesses you, it blesses the world."

I could see that Saxon and Angle might, one far day, be one. But Fey and Human? Would the Goddess pour clear and muddy waters together?

174

Then I saw Her in the distance, feet on earth, head above the clouds. She poured water from two jugs together, and the mingled stream ran upon the earth like down-pouring rain, and She thought nothing of it. Less than nothing. In the same way I myself might scoop water from a stream with no thought that tiny beings might live in it; or, if I thought it, I would not mind. The water beings lived their life, and I lived mine.

So far above us, away from us, the Goddess lives, even as She lives also within us. I shivered, and pulled myself back out of the vision.

"How?" I asked Merlin. "How will the Grail bless me?"

"You will bury it with me as a sacrifice. You will bury me as a sacrifice, and my Enchanter. Three of us together. Then you will be blessed and healed."

"Bury . . . Bury you?"

"In Counsel Oak. You know the great lightning rift in his side. In there. Me. Enchanter. The Holy Grail. Silence, Niviene. Mellias comes."

Turning, I saw the Otter approach like a breath of breeze, his small feet barely pressing grass. Carefully held in both hands, he brought water in a leaf-bottle.

"Merlin, little is hidden from Mellias. He has his own mysterious power."

Merlin tried to smile. "Not so mysterious. The greatest power in the world. He stole a spark of it from the Humans."

But Merlin spoke no more of burial, sacrifice or forgiveness while Mellias tended him.

⟞⟝❧⟞⟝

Under Counsel Oak his yellow leaves lay piled. Autumn sun smiled down between bare, massive branches. Mellias and I laid Merlin down at his feet and ourselves sank down to rest.

When he first glimpsed a smudge on the golden horizon, Mellias had said, "There's home!" Merlin had slumped back against me.

Together we swayed to the steady pace of the grey charger; and suddenly Merlin's blood flowed black over us both, soaking tunics and trousers.

I knew he had held back the bleeding by sheer power till now, when home was in sight; now we must make haste, or Merlin might never come to Counsel Oak alive.

Mellias galloped ahead to signal the Children's Guard to hold their poisoned darts. The grey charger paced steadily past harvesters and Midsummer Tor and on to East Edge. There, Mellias had gathered children willing to help us. They had a raft waiting for us in the river. I rode into forest shade and the Goddess embraced me.

Merlin had warned me, "Your mother will not be there." I had answered, "I know." I had known since I dreamed of her entering Counsel Oak. "No matter," Merlin gasped. "The Goddess will greet us." And with the forest air, with the rich smells of mushroom and nut, dead leaf and mold, Her arms came around us.

The children helped Merlin to the raft and took the charger in payment. We left him in their midst, small brown imps climbing his mane, dancing on his back and sliding down his sides. He was the largest, most docile animal they had ever seen. I hoped they would do him no harm. We turned the ponies loose.

I steadied Merlin on the raft and Mellias poled upriver, pushing through flocks of ducks and swans that hardly moved to let us pass.

When the Fey lay down their bones like autumn leaves, they wander alone into deep thickets. Their bones are seldom found. So had my mother wandered away while I busied myself with Arthur's Peace.

Merlin had a Human plan. Not for him the secret thicket, the lost bones remembered only by the Goddess. No. Merlin had come here to Counsel Oak at great pain and by great power to make the ancient tree his tomb, his memorial, such as Humans love.

With his last strength he crawled into the black cavern that lightning had carved long ago. He folded himself cross-legged, leaned his head back against the black wood and reached out skeletal hands. At the gesture, his blood leaked again. I had not thought the body contained so much blood as Merlin had shed.

"Enchanter," he whispered.

Mellias handed him the old harp. It seemed to leap like a child into his hands. He held it as though ready to play, and groaned, "Now. The Holy Grail."

I took the tarnished, battered dish from the saddlebag. A moment I held it, feeling the love it had absorbed over Human generations. Only the Goddess could know how many loving hands had heaped feasts upon it—or spread crumbs to look like feasts—and offered it to hungry families. Only She knew all the hands that had dipped into it, crumbled bones now.

I gave it to Merlin, who placed it to be his breastplate.

He whispered, "Children. Listen."

I found it very hard to lean over Merlin, feeling the approach of Death just behind me. Mellias must have found it harder. But we leaned, and listened.

Merlin mumbled, "Hermit Caleb gave us his nut mast in this Grail . . . cheerfully . . . keeping none for himself . . . Now I take this Holy Grail to the Goddess . . . for world-healing.

"Enchanter goes with me to the Goddess.

"I give my bones to the Goddess, who gave them.

"Niviene, my daughter. When your heart returns to you, your power will return in full. Go now to Arthur, as I have told you; and when you find Mordred, forgive me."

I said softly, "Merlin, whatever wrong you have done cannot be changed. It is in the past."

"Only remember, child, that I was not always wise."

"I will, Merlin."

"And remember that I love you."

Love. Forgiveness. These were hard concepts for me, who had remained steadfastly Fey. Perhaps Mellias understood them better.

"I loved you best," Merlin said, and closed his weary eyes. "Now . . . seal the cavern."

In my dream, when the Lady passed into the cavern it healed and sealed itself behind her. This time, in true daylight, Mellias and I had to seal it. Roughly, quickly, we piled leaves into and over the entrance. In only moments Merlin's bone-white face disappeared under yellow leaves. The Holy Grail still shone through. We covered that. Merlin's even fingers, resting on the harp strings, vanished last.

We stood back, panting slightly. Then Mellias turned, strode to the lake shore, and came back with an armful of mud caught in reeds. This he slapped over the leaves.

We finished the sealing with mud, and with earth dug with our hands, and over all we laid stones. (Later, unknown hands leaned one great flat rock across the cavern, such as Humans raise over a chief's grave.)

Gasping now, trembling from the work, we sank to rest under Counsel Oak. Otter Mellias seemed to sleep instantly. I lay awake, thinking over Merlin's last words.

Daughter, he had called me.

Merlin was a poet, and he spoke poetically. But in truth I had always felt for Merlin what I think a Human daughter feels for her father. The accident of our even-lengthed fingers formed a bond between us. Merlin was so often there as I grew up, standing like a shade tree over the Lady and me. I remembered him baking oat-cakes on stones while the Lady rocked small me in her lap, the three of us like a family. I remembered him carrying me into the forest after my first ride, when I could not walk.

I swallowed hard and my eyes blurred. If I thought more along this line I might weep, as I had wept in Arimathea Orchard.

But we Fey do not weep for the dead. We live in this moment, we sing this note of the Goddess' eternal song.

Mellias stirred and opened his eyes. "Niviene, we did all that he said."

"Yes, we did."

"Now we are free." Mellias' voice lilted. I turned to look at him.

For a long time now, Mellias had lived an almost Human life, among Humans. Now at last he owed nothing to Lugh, who had abandoned us; nothing to Merlin, who was dead; now he could stay forever in the forest and return to his true, Fey self.

I shook my head. "One more thing, Mellias. We must go to Arthur's battle."

"Not I."

That startled me. "You will not come?" Somehow I had assumed that Mellias would go where I went, like a hound.

"Not I," he repeated. "When Merlin ordered that, he was fevered. It makes no sense, Niv. What would you do in battle? Have you ever seen battle? By the Gods, I have! I will not go."

"There is something I must do there . . . I must forgive. That is what he said. Forgive."

Mellias made a gesture as of brushing debris off his tunic.

I thought that when he was a little rested he would change his mind. He would not let me go alone to this awful thing called Battle.

Counsel Oak rustled his leaves.

I looked up then into Counsel's bare branches, and I saw them crowded with ghosts. Like pale birds they perched on the branches, or swung from them, or hovered among them. Fey and Human, male and female, some naked, some trailing rich robes, they twittered softly, like birds heard afar.

And now I saw that some were Godly, towering so huge among the others and intertwined with them, that at first I had not seen them as separate beings at all. And some, small as bees, hovered on shimmering wings. And all of their misty eyes were bent, unwavering, on the mud-sealed cavern below.

At my shoulder, Mellias whispered, "What is it?"

I wet my lips to answer. "They are here. Merlin's friends."

Mellias moved closer to me. I felt him tremble.

Trembling myself, I searched the cloud of forms for one familiar face. If these great spirits came to greet Merlin, ancient and new-dead, would not the Lady be found among them?

I glimpsed what might be her old crone-face, peering under the wing of a giant form. A maiden that might be she—younger than I ever saw her—perched on a high limb—maybe the limb from which I had first spied Gwen, so long ago.

But I could not be sure of either phantom, and soon I gave up the search. This vision spread far beyond my private concerns, which lost themselves in it, like water dropped in the lake.

Now from the sealed cavern wisped a cloud. At first a thin trail of mist like breath on a frosty morning, it gathered strength and form till I thought even Mellias must see it. It drifted and bobbed and staggered, like a man stretching awake. Coldly it reeled through Mellias and me and brightened, turning a faint sunrise orange. It kicked free of earth and drifted slowly upward, curling like smoke among the ghosts and Gods gathered in Counsel's branches; and, as it reached them, they dissolved to mist themselves. And the cloud covered the old tree and hid it entirely; and the cloud rose and rose away, and Counsel Oak came slowly back into sight, trunk and covered cavern and bare, stretched branches; the sun looked down through the cloud, and it was gone.

I sighed. "They are gone," I told Mellias.

But we did not move.

Later we took off our clothes and waded into the lake. Suffering and death are contagious. Like sickness, they leap from one body to another. We had lived with Merlin's suffering for days, and now his death had touched us. We looked to the freezing water to cleanse us of contagion.

I swam far out and floated, looking back at Avalon Island. From the water I saw the trees bare or golden, and a pale smudge that was my mother's villa, now my den, and ancient Counsel Oak, that easily overtopped all the apple trees of Avalon.

A Merlin Song

And small Merlin said,
. . . "Under the fort two dragons lie.
Like Angle and Saxon they skirmish and vie,
As Saxon and Angle lie each beside
Waiting to learn what may betide,
What the Gods for this country may decide.
And while they wait they twist and fight
Like these your dragons, one red, one white."
So the child speaks, then looks around
As for the first time. The drum's heart-sound
For the first time he seems to hear.
He sees the knife poised; the Saxon Queen
Kneels at his side and lets him lean
On her, while torches sputter and flare
And King and Druid argue there.
The Druid commands, "You shall slay this child,
Mix with your mortar the blood of this child,
Whose father's unknown, of Hell or the wild!"
But Vortigern murmurs, "I'll have him taught
Druid and Christian way and thought,
Magic and medicine, seeing afar.
He'll be my kingdom's guiding star!"
So Vortigern murmured, as our bards sing . . .
But that star would shine for another king.

13

THREE QUEENS

Under the boughs of Counsel Oak, Mellias had said, "When Merlin ordered you to go to Arthur, he was sick. Fevered. What can you do there?"

Later, by my courtyard fire, he said, "Go, if you insist." And shrugged. Busily bent over, he cleaned the reed of his pipe.

My own cold desolation surprised me. Had I become—Gods forbid!—dependent on my Otter?

I said, "You know I am going into danger."

"I know that better than you do!"

"But you will not come." I was truly puzzled. All these years Mellias had been a shield at my back.

He straightened, laid the pipe aside and faced me across the small fire. "Niviene," he said gravely, "know this. When first I came to live on Apple Island, and you came back here from the Children's Guard, I desired you. You knew it."

I nodded. Dread prickled my stomach. Never had I heard Mellias' voice so heavy.

"One Flowering Moon after another, I waited for you. At first you danced with others. Then you did not even dance. So I found other partners."

"Aefa."

"True, I found Aefa. But it has never been as it would be with you. For you, Niviene, I traveled out into that terrifying kingdom."

"Not so! You went for the adventure!"

"Yes, when I was young. Niviene, we are no longer young. Have you noticed?"

I studied Mellias by gentle firelight. "You have not a grey hair on your head!" But wrinkles of anxiety had creased his face.

He continued. "I went for adventure, and for Lugh. Lugh was to me what a brother should be to a Human. Later, I went for you. To look after you. To be your . . . shield."

I broke gaze with him and looked down into the fire. I think what I felt was what Humans called shame.

"Niviene, I lived a long time among Humans. Longer than you, for I went out there earlier. You know, when you live among strangers you learn their language. You learn their thought, too.

"I never despised the Humans as you did, so I learned from them. I learned . . . love from them. I came to love Merlin, and Aefa, and you most of all."

(I remembered Merlin's words, painfully gasped by the stone table. "The holy power instructs our Mellias. He stole a spark of it from the Humans.")

I looked up to Mellias. "And yet . . . now I go into danger, you will not come."

"Listen, Niviene. In two days the moon will flower. I had hoped that this time you would be there, but if you are gone to Arthur's battle, never fear for me; I will find myself a merry companion, as I have done before.

"For years I have followed you like a hound and covered you like a shield. Now that is finished. We are home. Merlin is dead. Lugh has left us. Now let this Human folly die out of me! If you choose now to jump into a coracle and float back out there to a kingdom battle, that is your choice, for you. You shall not choose for me any longer. I, Mellias, choose to roll up in my otter skin robe and sleep for two days. Then I will dance, with you if you are there. Or with another. Then I will mend my nets and pick a few apples. I may dry them for winter, Human-style. I choose to return now to my true self and my true life, and forget all that has been, and all that fantastic, grim world out there. It can go about its business, and I will go about mine."

Never had Mellias spoken at such length before, or with such emphasis. Never had I seen him utterly humorless till now.

Faintly I murmured, "Merlin's last words. I must go."

"Then that is your choice. I do not fear for you. You do not know what you are going into, but you will survive it. True Fey are survivors." And Otter Mellias picked up his pipe, thrust it into his belt, and rose up away from my fire like silent grey smoke. I did not watch him go. Shivering with a strange chill, I fastened my gaze on the fire and willed to see Arthur. But the fire told me nothing.

Had the fire shown me a moment of what Merlin had called the Battle of Camlann, I might have rolled up and slept for two days like Mellias. Shivering beside the fire, I might have reconsidered his earlier words. "Have you ever seen battle? By the Gods, I have."

Mellias had seen battle, and he was not going. A prudent Fey would have considered this, and her tiredness; she would have asked herself what claim a dead man could have on her, that she should do his will.

But that night, and the next morning, I was not true Fey. I was not a heartless mage. I was . . . By the Gods, I acted like a bewitched Human woman!

Single-minded, I obeyed Merlin. Never before had I ventured into the kingdom alone. Alone now, I put on the warm woolen shirt and trousers my mother had left for me, and my Child Guard invisible cloak. (Mellias' crystal hid, as always, under my shirt.) Alone, I packed a pouch of nuts, climbed into a coracle and poled downstream, following Merlin's directions.

So it was that I came to crouch in the coracle in a forest of reeds, while the Battle of Camlann raged on the bank.

The sun looked calmly down on this amazing horror and passed on his way. Buzzards circled slowly, patiently waiting. Sun and buzzards had seen Human battle before. They did not have to smell it, or hear it close to, as I did.

The screams of men and horses rent the air, to a constant accompaniment of groans, grunts and the clash of steel. Fecal matter and blood stank together. My head throbbed and I retched, though my stomach had long since emptied itself. Most of the fighting took place out of my sight, over the bank; but now and then a desperate pair of antagonists, mounted or on foot, came rolling or sliding down the bank and fought in the water, which now burbled pink through the reeds. Three human corpses and a dead horse clogged the reeds near me. Looking up I saw the battle-aura dark as a storm-cloud in the sky, and the Morrigan Crow circling among the patient scavengers. That huge black bird screaming blood-lust and delight could only have been She.

Why these men sacrificed their healthy bodies I could not imagine. Most of them would live no differently under King Mordred than under King Arthur. They fought no Saxons here, but their own Angle brothers, with whom they were drinking ale a moon ago. It was as incomprehensible to me as the game of Tournament Lugh used to play with the village boys. Now and then a boy would fall and break a leg, or narrowly escape blinding, and Elana and I would marvel at their folly. So now I marveled at the folly of battle, where a healthy man was killed every moment for no clear reason.

I crouched hidden in the coracle, safe except from a direct hit by a combatant rolling down the bank, and listened, smelled, retched and ached. Rightly had Mellias asked, What will you do there?

But wait. The roar of battle was less. The shouts, groans and clashes sounded farther away. As when a thunderstorm draws away, and thunder growls and mutters and sinks into silence while lightning still flashes, so the battle seemed to ebb from the bank.

The hopeful buzzards circled lower.

Just as I began to think of climbing the bank and peering over, a knight came reeling along, pursued by two others; and I crouched low and pulled reeds close before me.

The fugitive was small, slight, armed in black. A black plume dangled askew from his helmet; blood drenched his left side. A giant followed him closely, swinging a sword that shone through all the blood that slimed it. This man hardly bled, though armor and tunic were shredded. He must have been wounded, yet the sheath that slapped against his thigh was free of blood, and so were the remnants of his cuirass and tunic.

(And Merlin said, "This is the magic sword, Caliburn, who always draws blood. And this is his sheath, even more precious, for he who wears this enchanted sheath, however wounded, will never bleed.")

I blinked, remembering the song in the tavern, the listening giants and the spell that Merlin laid on them, so that they forgot their grievances and rallied again in their hearts to Arthur and his Peace.

That part of the song about the sheath was here proven. Here came Arthur, whom I had twice loved, who had cost me my power and my brother, who had given me a son he never knew; here came this proud giant, staggering under wounds that should have stretched him dead by now, but shedding no blood, swinging magic Caliburn at his enemy nephew.

And behind him, some way behind, blundered a blood-blinded giant, also swinging his sword. I could not decide which man he meant to fight, but it did not matter. He reeled and stumbled and fell over corpses, so it seemed the first two would finish their business before he caught them up.

On the bank just above me Mordred paused, wheeled slowly around and faced Arthur. Neither man carried a shield. Each raised sword high above head with both hands and rushed upon the other.

Had I been a bard hiding in the rushes, I could have sung this duel at feasts and fairs for the rest of my life. I could have lived on this duel. I knew exactly how it should sound, where the harp should thrum, how to sing the tremendous clash of swords; how the heroes swayed, struck and fell and rose again; how they drove one another back and forth along the bank; how nothing ever grew again where their bloody feet pressed; how forever after this stretch of bank would be barren and lifeless. One struck the other to his knees and the other pulled the one's feet from under him. They rolled in bloody mud, dropping swords, groping for knives. A fine song this would be, with a chorus about the river running red.

Together as one they found their knives, drew their knives, drove their knives each through riven cuirass and chest.

Together as one they rolled apart, writhed, lay still.

The giant follower ran up and bent over Arthur. He crashed to his knees and cradled Arthur in his arms. He was Bedevere.

I found myself climbing the bank and stood between Arthur and Mordred, and looked from Arthur to Mordred.

Both still breathed. As I turned his way, Mordred opened a narrow red eye and croaked. I leaned down to listen, and heard, "M-Ma, M-Ma," like the bleat of a separated lamb.

I knelt down and took Mordred's even-fingered, gloved hand. Low I bent to hear his bleats, and I felt power rise tingling up my spine as though it had never slept; I sank down through Mordred's tight, white face and through his skull and into his mind.

The iron door that had been locked in his mind stood open. Through the door I saw apple trees, summer sun, sparkling water. Avalon Island. But I was seeing it from low to the ground. Ferns brushed my face.

I, tiny Bran, stumbled over roots and rocks, calling to my Ma. She strode ahead, not looking back. Her long black braid swung down her back. A reed basket bounced against her shoulder. Her stride rustled no undergrowth, snapped no twig. Silent, she disappeared behind a giant apple tree.

Huge grey trees bent down to stare at me. Something stepped in a thicket. I cried, "M-Ma!" fell over a rock and landed in a bawling heap.

Ma appeared again. Like a doe, she seemed to grow from the apple tree, peering around it.

I was not really crying, just bawling, so I saw her clearly. I saw her wry, disapproving face, the thin lips twisted. I knew she did not like noise. I knew if I bawled again she would disappear, and leave me alone with the staring trees and the thing that stepped in the thicket.

I tempered my bawl to a whimper. "M-Ma!"

She shrugged. Swift and silent, making not a whisper of sound, she came back and stood over me. I saw her like a tree, looking down her deerskin tunic at me.

I snuffled. I hurt very badly, much worse than from a fall over a rock.

My mother knelt down before me. Her warm brown arms came around me. I buried my face in her breasts that smelled of sweet milk.

Sun shone, cuckoo called. I lay content in M'ma's arms, and she stroked my hair. And now I did not hurt any more.

I, Niviene, drew back out of Mordred, to myself. I was Niviene, Lady of the Lake. I held my son Bran in my arms; his blood drenched my breasts and belly; I felt his heartbeat, erratic and feeble, against my own. I had pushed off his helmet and was stroking his black, soaked curls, and murmuring to him.

He convulsed, and I held him. He died and I held him, murmuring to him, till I felt the spirit rise away out of him.

Mordred was free. This was a bad life I had given him. My little Bran had not been himself since he was small. He did not remember being my Bran till a moment ago, when death broke down the iron door in his mind. Now he was free.

And I had stood in his brain with Death. Through his eyes I had seen the Goddess, disguised as myself. How could I ever fear again?

Without haste I laid the body down. I took the small, gloved hands with the even fingers and crossed them on the breast. I thought forgiveness to Merlin. He had not known.

Now that Mordred/Bran had passed, as Merlin had passed, I was free. Let buzzards strip his once-beloved bones. I sat back on my heels and looked around me.

Sir Bedevere still knelt by Arthur, who still breathed. Caliburn's magic sheath could no longer dam the tide of blood from his savage wounds. He bled richly from side and thigh and breast.

Bedevere sobbed.

Arthur gasped, "Caliburn. Give him to the Lady. Throw him in the river."

And Merlin said, "The Lady of the Lake gives you Caliburn to drive the Saxons from our land. The day you fail your people, young king, She will require him back from you."

I stood up.

Bedevere had been killing men all day. His small aura shone red against the storm-clouded air. I approached him warily, holding out empty hands. I said, "Bedevere, I am the Lady of the Lake. Give Caliburn to me."

Bedevere looked up at me through blood and tears. He saw a boy, someone's squire—disheveled, blood-smeared and dripping from the river. He looked beyond me.

I said, "Bedevere, I am the Lady of the Lake. Mage Merlin and I gave Caliburn to Arthur. Now I require him back."

Arthur gave a heave and flop, like a landed fish. "Give," he croaked. "Give Caliburn . . . to the Lady." He tried to lift Caliburn himself, but could not.

Bedevere took up the sword. Once again he looked beyond and around me, seeking the fabled "lady."

I stood close enough to grasp the hilt myself; also close enough to take the blade through my chest. Patiently I held out my hands and said, "Bedevere. Give me the sword." And I added a short, sharp Fey phrase that Humans know from old songs.

At that, Bedevere's wavering gaze focused on me. Slowly, he gave Caliburn into my hands.

A shock ran up my arms and down my sides.

Caliburn pulsed power. I had always assumed the Caliburn story was one of those Fey inventions that gather power from Human minds, like the tales of cloud-castles and hundred-year nights and transformations, tales that we invent to safeguard our forests from invasion.

But Caliburn was truly an ancient weapon, magicked long ago with lasting, binding spells. Who the magician was—Fey, Human, maybe one of those ancients who raised Morgan's Hill—I could not guess; but I took the force of his—or her—magic in my hands, and almost dropped the sword.

To handle Caliburn I needed the sheath.

Arthur would be dead now without that sheath. But he lay close to death in any case. I pointed, mutely demanding. And Arthur struggled to speak. Bedevere hesitated, then took the sheath and handed it up to me. Quickly I slid Caliburn within.

Now the magic was muffled. The sheath had its own power, but it did not compare to that of the sword. I thrust the sheathed weapon through my belt and knelt with Bedevere.

Arthur's wounds burst open all together. With knife and teeth I ripped strips from my tunic to staunch the flood. Bedevere signed himself with the Cross and prayed aloud. Arthur's breath rattled.

Behind us the river slapped the bank. I looked over my shoulder. A boat came gliding through the reeds to bump the bank. A barge, carpeted, cushioned, poled by a small Fey woman, robed like a queen. Aefa. Beside her stood a proud Human woman, richly gowned. Her face and hair were veiled, but I knew her at once.

I said, "Bedevere, your prayers are answered."

Bedevere turned and stared. He crossed himself again and muttered, "The Witch!"

"She is your Lord's sister. If anyone in the world can heal him, she can. Lift him, Bedevere. Carry him to the barge."

Thank all Gods, Arthur had fainted. He never felt Bedevere gather him up in huge mailed arms, crushing and mangling his wounds, to stagger with him down the bank and deposit him on cushions that Aefa had spread ready.

I followed. Standing in the reeds, I asked Morgan, "Lady, where will you take him?"

She stared down at me through her veil. How did this ragged, blood-spattered boy dare speak to her, the royal witch? But after a thoughtful moment she chose to answer. "Tell his companions he goes to Avalon, the Isle of Apples, where the Lady of the Lake may heal him."

I said, "Morgan, I am the Lady of the Lake."

Aefa had bent over Arthur, staunching his wounds. Now she glanced up at me and cried, "Niviene!"

Morgan drew her veil away and looked at me again. "Why, yes," she said, bemused. "You are in truth Mage Niviene! Will you be host to us at Avalon and try to save my brother?"

I said, "Lady, I will." Though I knew that venture was hopeless.

"Then come with us."

I hesitated. Dark shadow-wings swept over the barge. Death might swoop to land there at any moment. Could I, true-born Fey, ride that narrow barge with Death?

I made to climb aboard but found myself grasped from behind by big, gauntleted hands and lifted onto the barge. Thus the giant Bedevere rendered his last, loving service to Arthur.

I thought of telling Morgan that her foster-son, my son, lay dead on the bank a few feet away. I thought of telling Aefa that. I immediately decided for silence. Even the most vicious Humans love. Morgan might leap overboard, splash ashore and keen over dead Mordred. Meantime, men were gathering along the bank, looking down at us. Arthur's life ebbed, moment by moment. We had no time to lose.

Clear of the reeds, Aefa paused in her poling to pluck a silken cape off the carpet and hand it to me. Gratefully I closed it over my drenched trousers and shirt. It held off some wind and lent me some dignity. Enough so that I heard a bard's voice call from the hillock where he had watched the battle, "Three Queens bear the King away!"

Now as we moved upstream into clear water I saw men all along the bank. Exhausted, bleeding men of both armies watched us pass, leaning on spears or sitting on earth. If they had come splashing out to stop us, we could hardly have resisted them. But they feared magic. And Arthur seemed to be dead. Quietly, they let us pass.

Over them swept the buzzards, waiting to feed. Among these the Morrigan Crow circled, rising, sinking, rasping her delighted blood-thirst. Two swans sailed over the barge and dropped into the river. One on each side, they swam beside us.

So, and in that manner, we left the Battle of Camlann and came to Avalon, with Arthur the High King near bloodless on Morgan's embroidered cushions.

A Counsel Oak Leaf Song

〜◦〜

From under rock let water rise
From root and leaf to wind and skies,
Bring the brew of earth and bone
Blood and beard, sap and stone
From soil to sky to sweet, rich rain,
Run under rock and rise again.

14

DANCE

⸎

Aefa says, "Niviene. I want to dance to the Flowering Moon tonight. Will you stay with Dana?"

Little Dana hears her name spoken and looks up. She sits square on the Dana mosaic in the villa entrance, plump, even-lengthed fingers spread on the colored pebbles. She smiles the flower-soft smile of babyhood, leans forward on her hands and rocks herself up on hands and feet.

Brooding on her, eyes only for her, I murmur, "I mean to dance tonight, myself."

Dana is Aefa's child. Aefa declares my son Bran to be her father. That makes me her grandmother, Arthur her grandfather, the Lady her . . . holy Earth! Her great-grandmother! This child has a lineage like any proud Human! Now, if I knew my father . . . but, as Aefa once said, no one knows their father.

Aefa cries, astonished, "You, Niviene? You want to dance?" And turns to me, even as little Dana pushes herself upright.

There she stands, swaying on soft, never-used feet, where her father had first stood up, where I had first stood up. I gasp. Aefa turns to look.

Dana plumps down hard on the pebbles and opens her mouth to wail. The villa rings with our delighted laughter.

Dana pauses, mouth open. She looks from Aefa to me and back to Aefa. Then she crows.

When I can speak again, I say, "Yes, I mean to dance tonight, and every Flowering Moon hereafter. I have missed far too many dances."

"But Niviene . . . your power . . ."

"What power I have will stay with me. What more power do I need?"

For the Saxons have not come. The terrible golden-haired savages have not driven our Angle neighbors into our forest. Now that Merlin cannot bring us word of the Human world, there is no word. I steal among the trees like any simple wild thing; like any Fey who never heard of Arthur, or of King Mark or of chivalry, Romans or Saxons. I think I have forgotten how to ride a horse.

I say to Aefa, "Who knows, I may yet sacrifice once more to the Goddess." My arms know once more the warm weight of a child. "I am not past it, you know."

Now, by the light of the Flowering Moon, I lift my white shift hip-high, sling my shoes around my neck and push out the coracle. I climb in and take up the pole as the first drumbeat throbs over the water.

A moon-shimmering path leads me straight across the Fey lake. Dark water slides by under the coracle. Somewhere about here, under me now, lies my young, drowned heart. That heart has been dead for fifteen years; I cannot resurrect it. Yet ever since Dana's birth I have felt a similar, tentative presence about to beat, almost beating, in my breast.

Somewhere about here, under me now, lies King Arthur, whom I loved. He died before we three queens reached the island. Here we drowned his bloodless body. The Angles had lost their defender that day. Humankind lost a great hero, of whom bards will sing forever. And I lost . . . my dangerous friend, my enemy lover.

Somewhere about here we also drowned Caliburn. I said, "This Caliburn has shed enough blood!" The sticky liquid coated him completely. My spirit ear still heard the shrieks of the Morrigan Crow. I dropped Caliburn down the lake with his master, sheath and all.

By then, Morgan knew that Mordred was dead. Her country was ruled by some new, unrelated king. She had no home back in the kingdom. She begged me, "Let me stay with you now, here in this blessed quiet."

I shrugged. "Whether you go or stay is not for me to say."

"If not you, who rules the Fey?"

"No one rules the Fey."

As I said those words an invisible, unguessed burden slipped from my shoulders into the lake. I never knew I carried it, but I felt it fall. It lies down there now with Arthur, Caliburn and my young heart.

My new heart beats now with the soft drum across the water. I feel it pulse. It flowers like a red moon in my breast, under Mellias' crystal.

This resurrection, this resurgence, is not Fey. This springtime spirit is a Human trait, like the courage I have had to learn, like love.

Long I have suspected I might have Human blood. I did not want to believe it. But now, poling under the Flowering Moon, I invite the thought into my mind. Merlin said that life is one, that Human and Fey will be one, some day. Maybe they are one in me, tonight. Maybe those two streams have always flowed in my blood. One of them I rejected, out of . . . Human? . . . pride and fantasy. No more. I am Fey enough to accept truth when I see it.

Close now, I hear a familiar pipe trill. Mellias and I have not spoken since he said no to me. I have watched him from hiding, as I did in girlhood. I have listened to his distant pipe and warmed his crystal in my fingers.

The coracle whispers into tall reeds, bumps land. That inward stir, that newborn movement is my heart, beating.

A Human hunter would not call this path a path. If one, sharper-eyed than most, noticed it, he would think it a hare's trail. It leads me indirectly, with much pausing and changing course toward the fireglow.

The drum beats. The pipe lilts and trills around the rhythmic sound. From Mellias' dangling crystal, a soft, eager warmth spreads through my body, the same warmth I last felt with Arthur in a moonlit meadow. The trail leads around a great white beech into the dancing glade.

I lean against the beech, white shift pressed to white bark. "Invisible," I scan the glade.

Silhouettes against the snapping fire, dancers whirl softly past. One startling, tall figure skips like a root-freed sapling, gems winking back firelight from flying hair and waving hands. Morgan still haunts our forest. Aefa is a smaller, slower shadow. Perhaps she left Dana asleep nearby.

A lean, small fellow like a startled white buck comes leaping by, stamping and tossing his antlered head. His eyes gleam darkly, turning this way and that, searching me out where I stand invisible, white against white.

He snorts surprise and leaps out of the circle. Cautiously, he glances toward me, ready to spring away at a breath. Black braid swings across swinging white buckskin. Small dark hands reach for mine. Under his warm, swinging crystal my new heart swells warm. He grasps my hands and draws me, dancing, away from my sheltering tree.

My feet remember the steps.